Loch has chosen to forgo the usual paths that marked men, like him, complete to enter into Service and become fabulously wealthy. He has instead chosen to attend the University of North Carolina. His first year was quite extraordinary as he was drawn into a situation with the football team. That's where he meets another freshman, Marcus Battle, who becomes his boyfriend. Their relationship is just getting started as they begin their second year in school. Neither one of them knows how being separated in the summer will affect their relationship or what is about to come with the new year. Will Loch grow tired of the same man all the time or will Marcus put an end to the relationship in order to focus on his football dreams?

Cageless In College Sophomore Year
Copyright © 2020 Crawford Rhine
ISBN: 978-1-4874-3119-8
Cover art by Martine Jardin

Published by eXtasy Books Inc or
Devine Destinies, an imprint of eXtasy Books Inc

Look for us online at:
www.eXtasybooks.com or www.devinedestinies.com

Cageless In College
Sophomore Year

By

Crawford Rhine

CHAPTER ONE

It was the summer after my freshman year of college. Having experienced a weird sort of initiation by the football team at the beginning of my school year, I was now settled in and had finished the year on the Dean's List with a boyfriend who was on the football team. It had been a very good year for me.

When I was thirteen, at the precise moment of my birth, I was marked. A thick blue line appeared on my jaw line from my ear lobe to my chin. The mark, as it was called, was a sign in our world. It was rare and it marked me as special.

The world I grew up in was completely masculine. There were no women in our world, having been separated from the men for thousands of years. They had their own world to live in and procreation was accomplished by the use of catalogs. When the child was born, if it was male it was returned to the father in our world and if it was female, it stayed with the women.

The blue line on my face readily told anyone who looked at me that I was sexually attracted to men. This was both a blessing and a curse. The blessing was that I could have my pick of almost any man in the world. Even though NOMARs weren't sexually attracted to marked men, they had to have sex and in the absence of women, they were more than willing to fuck men who liked to be fucked.

The mark also gave me the opportunity to go to a special school only for marked men, called The Service Academy, and to enter a program called The Service. The Service brokered a deal between wealthy NOMARs looking for sex and marked men. A contract could be offered where the marked man would be offered a million dollars in exchange for becoming a sexual Servant to the wealthy NOMAR for one year.

It was a humiliating, degrading proposition, but one that could change your life. I loved being in control, and to give that up to take an almost random draw to see who would get to fuck me for the next year or two was unacceptable.

That lack of control paired with my confidence that I was going to make something of myself one day was the reason I decided to not attend The Service Academy. I stayed in high school and took a boyfriend each year, sometimes more for safety than for lust. I had also deferred my calling in The Service until after college. I had been told that this would probably severely reduce my chances at getting a call to service, but I wanted to have the college experience and I particularly wanted to go to the University of North Carolina.

I had started at UNC last fall and immediately got sucked into choosing a football player to date. Apparently, it was a source of pride among the Tarheel football team that they claimed every marked student as their own. As far as I knew, there were only two of us and the other marked man was a graduate student who had already been in service and was now independently wealthy, thanks to his Master's money.

I had slept around with a few of the football players until I decided on dating Marcus Battle. He was a quiet unassuming freshman when I met him, but his control over me made my blood boil. He had kept me at arms' length until I had selected him, but then we had fucked like our life depended on it and it was the greatest sex I had ever experienced.

Our first year at school had flown by in a blur of classes, sporting events, and sex. We'd spent spring break in Florida, where we were drugged at a beach party, but were able to escape before anything worse happened to us. Marcus and I finished the year on a high note, but the specter of the coming summer spent apart loomed large for us.

Marcus had encouraged me to take a lover over the summer so that I wouldn't be restless without him, but he did stipulate that it had to be someone older. He was still in control of me even though I was in South Carolina and he in Ohio.

The first thing I did when I got home from college for the summer was to convince my dad and brother to spend our vacation at Cedar Pointe Amusement Park in Ohio. We picked a date in early July and I immediately texted Marcus to tell him. He answered immediately and said that he and his father would join us there.

I read his text at least twenty times. It gave me a tingling sensation throughout my body, much like Marcus did when he was in the same vicinity as me. Marcus Battle and I had some kind of crazy physical connection that I had been unable to explain. Neither of us seemed to be able to get enough of the other and we genuinely enjoyed being with each other.

Unable to control myself, I went to the bathroom and whacked off while I visualized seeing Marcus at the amusement park this summer. He held such sway over me even from a distance that it was almost scary.

I had originally chosen to work for the city of Charleston during the summer, but a better offer had come from a tech firm so I decided on that instead. I had a few days off before my summer job at IBM started, so I unpacked my things, did laundry, and settled into the summer at my family's house. I missed Marcus terribly, but resigned myself to being without him for the summer. I had never *missed* someone before and I realized that my connection to Marcus Battle was unlike any other I had experienced before. It was grand and fast burning, but pain and pure pleasure at the same time. I couldn't wait for the end of the summer so that I could be with him again.

Marcus and I texted constantly and we loved sending each other pictures of things that we were experiencing. He called me every night at seven o'clock and checked in on me. I knew in my heart that this would soon start to dwindle as we got back into our lives for the summer and started working, but it was nice to have this routine the first week away from each other.

My dad and brothers could tell that something that had changed about me and that I was a different person than the one they had dropped off at college a year ago. To my family's credit, they tried to snap me out of my funk by taking me for ice cream after dinner, to the local drive-in on the weekend, and to my favorite restaurants. It only took me about four days to come out of my haze and rejoin the world, but it seemed like a much longer process when I was living it.

CHAPTER TWO

I started my summer job on a Monday, so I woke up early that morning and spent a lot of time getting ready. The letter I had received said to wear comfortable clothes including jeans and tennis shoes, so I was grateful that I didn't have to dress up. I wished I could have worn shorts, but the letter said that those were not allowed.

Driving south, I made the trip to the factory in less than fifteen minutes and spent at least that long trying to figure out which huge parking lot to park in. Once parked, I took the long walk to the front door. Gathered in a big sprawling lobby were twelve college kids dressed much like I was. I didn't recognize any of them and they were all curious about me, based on their intent stares.

A skinny nerdy guy in an ill-fitting suit soon appeared and explained that he was one of the trainers and that he was going to show us where we would work. He explained that this was a trial run of a program, and they were curious to see how it panned out.

We were led to a cavernous room dominated by a huge conveyor belt running through the middle of it. Individually, the trainer took us to a station beside the belt and explained what each job entailed. I was in the middle and he gave me a curious look as he led me to my station. The trainer explained that when the giant piece of machinery arrived at my section, that my job was to attach four screws into the body at locations shown on a picture laminated in my cubicle.

"You got it?" he asked.

"Yes," I answered with confidence.

He looked at me without saying anything for a few seconds. "Do you mind if I ask you a question?"

"No." I was used to being asked that question.

"You are marked?"

"I am."

"Then why in the world would you want to work here?"

I almost laughed out loud. "What do you mean?"

He leaned back slightly and gathered himself. "I mean, you are marked and good looking, so why didn't you enter The Service and make millions of dollars instead of working here?"

This was really none of his business, but I decided to indulge him. "I might, but I wanted to go to school first and that means that I have to work a summer job just like everyone else."

"Okay," he replied, probably in a manner that he used a lot to dismiss people when he didn't understand their actions.

"I think it is kinda cool that you are working in the trenches with the rest of us grunts," the guy across the belt from me said loud enough for me to hear. He was blond with wavy short cut hair and built like a fireplug—short and thick. He had nice arms and once the trainer left, we introduced ourselves.

I said, "Thanks for that."

"No problem."

"I'm Loch."

"Drake."

"Where do you go to school, Drake?"

"Marist . . . in New York. You?"

"Carolina. You wrestle or play football?"

"Football." He grinned. "How did you know?"

"You remind me of a good friend I have on the football team in Chapel Hill," I said, pulling up a stool and taking a seat.

It took all morning for the trainer to finish explaining our assignments. When he was finished, we took a tour of the factory and he showed us the break rooms, lunch rooms, and rest rooms. We were given an hour for lunch and all of us agreed to eat in the company cafeteria to save time.

The cafeteria was an interesting mix of people. There were a lot of the assembly line workers in casual clothes, nerdy guys in ties and short sleeved dress shirts that I imagined to be engineers or computer scientists, and then a small percentage of suits, who I guessed were management. The entire cafeteria seemed to come to a stop when we entered.

The employees weren't used to seeing college kids in their midst and the fact that one of them was marked created quite the buzz. We all sat together and told each other about what we were supposed to do on the assembly line. We eventually all learned where everyone went to school and lived. A guy named Chaz also went to UNC and said that he had seen me in class and walking on campus, but I had no recollection of him at all. He seemed nice enough and we talked about Chapel Hill for quite a while.

After lunch the assembly line started and we were all very anxious to get our parts right. It didn't take long to see that this was going to be a very boring waiting game for me. The conveyor belt had to be stopped constantly because either the kids at the beginning didn't do their jobs correctly or they needed more time to finish it before it moved away from them.

I spent the next four hours bored out of my mind. Drake and I talked through our frustration and by the end of the day, I had only screwed my screws into one machine. It was pretty sad and I saw no way that IBM could make money off of our line.

My family went out to dinner to celebrate my first day on

the job. I told my dad and brother about what a waste of time it was and my father responded with, "Well, I guess you know now that you don't ever want to have to do that kind of job for a living."

Dad was exactly right about that. My second day was almost as bad as the first one, but we were able to produce five completed machines. On Wednesday, we reached five machines right before lunch and then the line broke down. They sent us to lunch early and when we got back, it still wasn't fixed.

Our workroom was full of engineers, mechanics and a few suits when we returned from lunch. The twelve of us college kids hung back out of the way and watched as the rest of them tried to figure out the problem. A little later, the heavy door to our room opened and a tall man in a striking black suit entered. He was followed by several other suits carrying clipboards and reports.

I studied him, instantly thinking he was someone of importance because of the way he carried himself and the way everyone else acted towards him. He was probably in his fifties, but looked in shape under his dark suit. He was bald, but had a striking white goatee. He passed by us with just a curt nod of his head. I noticed that he had a straight long nose and very active eyes that took in everything as his body carried him forward.

This sense of confidence radiated from him and filled up the room. I was turned on by that more than anything and found myself shifting uncomfortably from foot to foot, trying to hide my hardening cock. Drake noticed my predicament and seemed to immediately put the pieces together, although he didn't say anything at the moment.

We had a long time to wait, because they never could get the belt to work again. They sent us home early and told us it would be repaired by the next morning. Some of the college kids decided to go out for a drink and invited me along. I made sure it was an upscale place and that there would be a group of us before I agreed to go. I was always vigilant about getting caught in the wrong place unprotected.

Someone picked a restaurant close to the factory that had a big bar, so we each drove there and re-convened. As soon as I entered the bar, I saw him. Seated at the bar across from me was a tall dark hunk of a man. His dark hair was slightly receding and I guessed his age to be around thirty. He wore a grey t-shirt that showed off tremendous arm muscles and hinted at a magnificent chest. His dark beard was longer in the goatee than on the sides, as if he had shaved the sides this morning, but his facial hair was so fast-growing that it soon filled in again.

The man watched our group with interest and when he noticed my mark and the fact that I was staring at him, he gave a slight nod. I liked that. Most guys would be cocky, smirk or come right over. I smiled and looked away from him to order a drink.

Several guys tried to come over and talk to me during the night, but I rebuffed them all. The boys were curious about how I handled all the guys at UNC, seeing for the first time what a marked guy had to deal with on a daily basis. I told them all about the football players' dating game and my selection of Marcus.

When I looked across the bar again, the dark-haired guy was gone and had been replaced with some loser in a suit. I felt a pang of disappointment, but quickly rallied. I finished my drink, said my goodbyes, and headed out to the parking lot.

He was waiting for me when I exited the front door. Dark and dangerous looked every bit the part as he leaned against someone's car, smoking a cigar. I almost stopped walking when I saw him, but slowed down instead.

"Hey," I said awkwardly.

He took a long pull on his thick cigar and eyeballed me. Pulling the stogie out of his mouth between his thumb and pointer finger, he spit on the sidewalk and then looked up at me with dark eyes.

"I thought you might have left," I said to him.

"I was going to go, because I saw you dismissing all of those idiots bothering you." His voice was deep and gravelly which made me wonder how many of those cigars he smoked a day.

"So, why didn't you?" I asked, deciding to challenge him.

"I don't know. A guy like me doesn't get a chance with . . . a guy like you, so I thought I would smoke one and see what happens." He took another long draw off of his cigar.

"I'm Loch."

"Travis," he said as he reached his hand out to shake mine.

I could tell by Travis' big rough hands that he was some type of manual laborer. It was probably where his huge biceps had come from.

"You a college kid?" he asked.

"Yeah. How'd you know?"

He nodded towards the bar with his head and said, "Your kind is not hard to spot."

"What do you do Travis?"

"Construction." He took another deep draw off of the cigar and blew the smoke out. "I got boys at home. I want them to go to college one day. Be better than their old man."

"You have sons?" I asked, suddenly very interested in him.

"Two," he said proudly.

"How old?"

"Johnny's five and Sherman is seven."

"Wow! Little men, huh?"

"They are. You like kids?"

"I do. I like daddies even more," I said flirtatiously.

His demeanor went lusty in a heartbeat. "What can you do for daddy?"

"Everything," I said, my voice all breathy. I hadn't flirted with anyone new in almost a year, since Marcus and I decided to date. It was wonderful and exciting, but it felt wrong. I knew that Marcus had encouraged me to take an older lover when we had left each other for the summer, but it still felt wrong.

But in a naughty good way. Hell, Marcus Battle practically commanded you to let this guy fuck you. This is what he wants. It was easy to tell myself that — to give myself permission to do whatever I wanted. Maybe Marcus did know me as well as he purported.

Maybe he was right, that this was what I needed to feel normal. *I reject that.* If that thought was true, then all I needed was a good hard fucking from any NOMAR. What I needed was a good hard fucking from Marcus Battle. But what Marcus was correct about was that a good hard fuck kept me even. It wasn't what I needed and it wasn't from who I needed it to be from, but it would help me think straight.

"Come on, boy. Come home with daddy," Travis said, while throwing down his cigar butt and stepping on it with his construction boots. His voice was so husky with lust that I practically was creaming my jeans already.

"Not with your boys home," I said at once.

"They are with their grandpap. That's why I could stop for a beer."

"What's your address?" I had already texted my family that I had stopped for drinks with my co-workers. Now, I would text the address to myself, so that if something foul happened, they would see where I had gone by pulling up my phone records.

Travis told me the address and I put it into my phone. "Now, don't make me punish you, boy. Get into my truck."

11

I loved his dirty talk and attempt at command, but I had to be smarter than the average nineteen year old. "I'll drive and follow you."

He dropped his tough-guy persona for a second and asked, "Is this really going to happen?"

"If you mean, am I going to come to your house, suck your big cock, and let you fuck my tight hole as many times as you want, then this is definitely happening, daddy," I teased him, right before turning and heading for my car.

CHAPTER THREE

Travis didn't live far from the restaurant where we had met. I followed his truck to a quiet cul-de-sac and into the driveway of a small, unassuming house. He emerged from his truck and waited for me to park.

I locked my car and headed up the driveway. Travis headed to the front door and unlocked it. He held the door open for me and I stepped into a modestly furnished house. There were toys and old newspapers lying about on the carpet of the living room, but besides that it looked pretty well-kept.

I turned around and Travis was right behind me. Lifting my hands onto his broad shoulders, I asked, "What would daddy like me to do first?" I rubbed my knee into the crotch of his jeans and felt his already-hard cock.

"Stop talking, boy, and wrap your lips around this," he said in his deep voice as he unzipped his jeans and pulled a nice-sized cock out.

I dropped to my knees on the carpeted floor and sucked him into my hot mouth. Travis' cock was nowhere near as thick and long as the one swinging between my boyfriend's legs, but it tasted musky and sweaty which was delicious to me.

His cock head was a small round mushroom on the end of a thicker shaft. Running my tongue all over that small head, I explored his piss hole and the seam where the shaft connected with the head. I plunged my mouth down onto as much of his cock as I could get around the fabric of his bunched-up jeans.

I hated fighting with denim and zippers to get to my man's dick.

Travis moaned in pleasure above me as he guided my head with a large rough hand on the back of my head. After another minute, he pulled his cock out of my mouth and said, "Not so fast, boy. You want to know what this big cock feels like punching up inside you, don't you?"

"Yes, daddy," I said, looking up to him. Truthfully, I did, so the script wasn't far from the action.

"Get to the bedroom," he ordered me, like I was one of his kids who were in trouble.

I scrambled up just as he grabbed the nape of my neck and escorted me down the small hallway. He pushed me forward into a darkened doorway before flipping the light switch, revealing a very small bedroom with a very large bed dominating it. Travis closed the door, sat down on the bed, and reached for a partially smoked cigar in an ashtray on his nightstand.

"This is the only room I smoke in," he told me.

I had figured as much because the tobacco smell was very strong in this room.

"Strip for daddy. Show me what you've got to offer, boy."

He was busy lighting his stogie, but he kept one eye on me the whole time as I pulled off my shirt, unbuttoned my pants, and kicked my tennis shoes off. I made it slow and seductive, which was hard for me to do because his thick cock was still sticking out of his fly and it was drooling pre-cum heavily.

Flicking my socks off, I watched as Travis leaned back and took a long drawing pull off of his cigar and watched me intently. I faced him, hooked my thumbs into the elastic band of my underwear, and pushed it to my knees. Travis' lips parted and he slowly blew smoke out. As I bent down to pull my underwear off, I slowly turned so that he got a spectacular look at my ass.

"Fuck me," Travis said gruffly.

"I'm getting ready to, daddy."

He took a big puff of his cigar and said, "Come take daddy's boots off, boy."

I walked over to the bed and knelt down beside Travis' legs. It took me a minute to figure out how his boots were tied, but I soon was pulling them off. He wore heavy work socks under them and I yanked those off as well. His feet didn't even compare to Marcus' cute dogs, so I didn't give them a second thought.

Standing up, I carefully grabbed the hem of his black t-shirt while he leaned forward to allow me to pull it over his head. I was delighted to see a broad, muscled chest covered in thick black hair.

"This is a real man's chest, daddy," I said, nearly salivating over it.

"I'm glad that you like it, boy. Suck daddy's nipples for him."

Leaning over him, I ran my hands all through his chest hair as my tongue flicked out over his small dark nipples, making them harden instantly. His nipples contracted and the tips projected, begging to be sucked. I gave into their demands and sucked one of them hard, biting and nibbling them gently with my teeth.

Travis moaned as he clenched his cigar butt in his teeth. I worked the first one over before moving onto the next one, giving it the same royal treatment. I started to massage his erect cock with one hand as I sucked his nipples. Straightening back up, I looked down to see that my hand was coated in his man-goo. I held my hand up so he could see his pre-cum coating it before I raised my hand to my mouth and licked it clean.

"God damn," Travis whispered.

"You ready to fuck me, daddy?" I asked as I lay down on

the bed beside him and stretched out like a lazy cat.

"Been ready," he growled, coming off of the bed and approaching me.

I pulled my legs up onto my chest and exposed Travis' final destination to him. His eyes dilated and he quickly shucked his jeans and boxers onto the floor. Travis never took his eyes off of my ass hole as he grabbed a bottle of lotion off of the dresser behind him and lubed up his hot unit.

"Give it to me, daddy. Give it all to me," I encouraged him. Closing my eyes, I held onto his oversized biceps as he pushed against my tight puckered hole and penetrated me.

"Tight as fuck," he grunted above me, causing me to open my eyes and watch him as he pushed inside of me.

"Fuck that tight hole open, daddy." I was disappointed that he didn't complete me like Marcus did, but at the same time, I was glad for it. I wanted no one to compare to my Marcus.

Travis bent over me, tenting himself with his big arms and began to fucking tear me up. He was good at fucking and had a lot of energy for a thirty-year-old who had worked all day, but he couldn't keep it up for long.

"Fuck," he hissed with a clenched jaw. Travis was biting the end of his cigar so hard that I wondered if it might break off and fall on me while I was being fucked.

"Fucking me so deep, daddy."

Travis continued to slam his big joint into me until he arched his back and pumped hot cum straight into my anal channel. He grunted with each ropy strand of cum that he shot into me.

When he finally rolled off of me, Travis lay on his back, breathing hard. I ran my hand across his sweaty chest and told him how much I had enjoyed it.

"It was amazing!" Travis said. "It's a once in a lifetime opportunity."

"I hope it's not just once," I teased.

"I'll be ready to go again in a minute. I'm going to go grab us some bottles of beer and then we'll see." He pulled out of me and left me with that terrible, empty feeling.

Putting my legs down and stretching them, I watched Travis' naked hairy ass as he left the bedroom. It was a good fuck, but it made me miss Marcus even more than I had before. But I did feel less on edge, more like myself than I had in a while. *Maybe Marcus had hit on something after all . . .*

"That was amazing," Travis said from the doorway. He held two bottles of beer and looked amazing, like a black bear approaching a trash can.

"It was really good," I agreed.

He walked to the bed and handed me a bottle. I greedily gulped it down and watched him do the same.

"So, how long you home from school, Loch?"

Oh, shit. This was not the way I wanted this to go. I could tell from his question and his sudden use of my name that this had changed for him. I decided to be honest and upfront with Travis.

"I'm home until early August, Travis, but this is kinda like a one-time deal. We're just having some fun, aren't we?"

I saw the cloud of disappointment cross his face and then a look of resignation appear. "Yeah, we're just having some fun," he repeated. I could tell that he didn't really mean it.

Feeling badly for him, I leaned down and sucked his sloppy cock into my mouth. It only took a few long drawing pulls on his dark sausage to get him back up hard again. Travis snapped out of his funk almost immediately, based on his enthusiastic groans.

When he was rock-hard again, I stopped blowing him and asked, "How would daddy like to enjoy me this time?"

"You're such a good boy," he said, stroking my hair. "I want you where I can hold onto you."

I wasn't sure what he meant by that at first, but when I saw him back up towards the headboard and prop himself on the pillows in a sitting position, I knew he wanted me to sit on his lap.

Standing up on the bed, I straddled Travis' lap and lowered myself down onto my knees. I faced him because I refused to get fucked in the same position that Marcus and I had come to call our own.

"I won't need lube this time, daddy. Your big load of hot cum inside me will make your big cock slide easily into me."

Travis let out a loud groan from deep inside his chest as he guided my ass down onto his harpoon. He slid into place inside me and I arched my back as the hot column of flesh seared its way into my depths.

I felt a pain on my chest and my eyes flew open. Shockingly, I saw Travis with his head on my chest and his lips wrapped around one of my nipples. He was sucking it hard and my instinct was to pull away from him, but instead when he switched to my other nipple, I pushed it into his hot hungry mouth.

The throbbing prick in my ass was insistently keeping time like a metronome set on high speed. Travis hungrily sucked on my nipples like he needed them to breathe. His hot mouth and prickly beard had my cock rock hard in no time and all I wanted now was to be fucked hard and to achieve my own release.

It became quickly evident that Travis had other plans in mind. He moved his mouth from my nipples to my collarbone and then to my neck. He wrapped his hairy muscled arms around my waist and back, holding me in place so that he could devour me with his unrelenting mouth.

I had never experienced this type of intimacy with anyone before, not even Marcus. NOMARs were not prone to do the things that marked men were, so I had never had my nipples sucked or felt a tongue as lusty as Travis'.

Turning up the intensity even more, Travis pulled me closer to him and put his tongue on my neck. He sucked on the large veins under my skin and even sucked my Adam's apple into his hot mouth. His hairy face continued to tickle the sensitive skin of my neck as his large rough hands ran over my exposed body.

It was sensory overload for me and the thought that his hot mouth might be on mine in a minute was almost more than I could take. I felt my body respond in the only way it knew to be able to relieve the pressure.

"I'm gonna come, daddy," I said, my voice breathy and sounding disconnected from my body.

"Let daddy see it, boy," Travis commanded gruffly.

I leaned back, supported by his hand while his other hand wrapped around my throbbing shaft. It was all the stimulation that I needed as my body released its sweet juice.

Groaning, I watched as my cock shot strand after strand of ropy cum onto Travis' big hand. He held that hand right in front of my piss hole and collected almost all of my hot spunk.

My ass muscles clamped down onto the cock that had taken up residence inside me. My climax had made my ass a lot tighter. I could feel my ass milking and squeezing Travis' prick from base to tip.

"That's a good boy. Daddy is proud of you, son." Travis rocked us which ground my ass down onto his pole even more. He held up his cum-filled hand to my mouth and said, "Daddy wants you to show him how you eat your favorite food, boy."

I immediately reached for his hand and pulled it to my mouth. Using my tongue, I scraped all of the still hot cum off of his palm and into my mouth.

Travis stroked my neck with his other hand. "Let daddy see you swallow it, boy."

I swallowed and felt his fingers follow the course of the cum as it went down my esophagus. Licking more off of his hand, I repeated the whole procedure and saw that Travis was very happy with me. Once I had his hand clean, I continued to lick and suck on his fingers like they were his cock and felt his dick harden even more in response.

"I'm going to fucking tear you up now, boy!" he said enthusiastically as he moved his hands to my ass cheeks, spread them apart, and then fucking railed me out.

This fuck reminded me of Marcus and I realized that I missed my partner terribly. I started to remember things that he had said to me at different points in our freshman year together and I suddenly got very sad. I missed him more than I ever thought I could.

I had promised him to continue working out, but I had not done that one single time yet. Maybe this fuck would qualify. *I don't think so!*

Recommitting myself to Marcus Battle, I rode Travis and looked forward to calling Marcus from the car on my way home.

CHAPTER FOUR

The next day I joined a gym down the street from work which was recommended by a lot of the college guys with whom I worked. After training with Burns for a year, I knew what I needed to work on each session in the gym, so I wasted no time in getting to it.

During the hour workout, I ran through the whole conversation from the night before that I had with Marcus, telling him about Travis. He had taken the news well and agreed with me that he probably was not the one to keep me busy this summer. I had heard a certain note to Marcus' voice that concerned me and I wasn't sure if it was jealousy, or longing, or disappointment. He assured me that he was okay and that I was doing exactly what he wanted me to do, but there was still something nagging at me.

My workout was pretty uneventful that first day, except that at the end, as I was headed to the showers, I saw the big boss from work seated at the curling machine. His biceps were huge and his grey t-shirt was dark with sweat. I stopped in my tracks for a second and took in his whole body while I had the chance.

The head guy's thighs were cut and defined as they braced his body under the machine. He wasn't a great looking guy, but he certainly kept himself in the best shape possible and had a certain sex appeal that I found very attractive.

Suddenly, I realized that he could see me in the mirror and I looked up in panic. He wasn't looking at me and I chastised myself for even thinking that he would be. I headed to the lockers, masturbated in the shower to the thought of that powerful man on top of me, got dressed, and headed home.

And so my days went by. I would occasionally see the big boss in the gym or at work, but he never once looked my way. Travis would occasionally text me to see if I had changed my mind about him, but I had not. I enjoyed my texts and calls with Marcus, but could feel our connection eroding with time and distance.

I must have fallen into some kind of funk, because my dad and brothers proposed that we go to eat Japanese hibachi on Saturday night. That was my favorite meal and I had not expected them to offer it up. They seemed excited by the thought of it and said that a new classy restaurant had opened near us in North Charleston. I found myself looking forward to something besides being with Marcus again.

The new restaurant was different from all other Japanese hibachis I had ever visited. Usually they cram a whole bunch of people at a cooking station and a chef prepares all the food at once. At Sugiyama, each party sat at their own table with a small hibachi grill, and a personal chef came over and cooked just for you. You could try whatever he was cooking or ask him to cook something special for you.

The clientele certainly was higher-class as well. I saw a bunch of guys in suits and wondered how many of them were conducting business over the hibachi grills. Our chef had just arrived when I looked up and saw three guys walk in, following one of the hosts. The man in the lead was the big boss from my work.

I found it a little curious that I was constantly seeing my boss everywhere I went and I watched in fascination as he was shown to his table. Once again, he was totally focused on what he was doing and totally unaware of me. Studying the two guys with him, I guessed that one was near his age and the other half his age. They resembled him but really were cookie cutter versions of each other, so I assumed the older one was Mr. Lewellyn's brother and the younger one was his nephew.

Soon, they were seated outside of my range of vision, so I went back to watching our chef and telling him what I wanted to eat. We had just finished eating and dad was paying the check when I heard my name called.

Looking up from my phone quickly, I saw the big boss standing right in front of me with his two friends.

"Your name is Loch, isn't it?" His voice was deep and smooth.

"Yes-yes, Sir," I stammered as I got to my feet. *How did he know that?*

"I don't think we have officially met, Loch. I'm Mr. Lewellyn and I run the factory that you are working for this summer while you are on break from Carolina."

How did he know that? "Nice to meet you," I said, grasping his extended hand. His hand was soft but the grip was firm and powerful.

"These are your father and brothers?"

"Yes," I said, noticing that my father had returned to the table. I introduced my family and then he did the same. The older guy with him was his brother, Richard, and his nephew, Ryan, just as I had thought. They both had dark hair that they kept shaved close to their heads and dark eyes framed with handsome faces.

My dad shook Mr. Lewellyn's hand enthusiastically and told him how much he appreciated him hiring me for the summer. To my horror, my dad began to tell Mr. Lewellyn how much it would help pay the bills.

"We're proud to have him. I have noticed his excellent work at the factory and even seen him at the gym." Mr. Lewellyn's dark gaze burned into my green eyes.

"That's nice to hear," my dad said, rubbing my back

proudly.

"Loch, I'm sorry to interrupt your time with your family, but I have a special project that I wondered if you might be interested in exploring. Can you come by my office first thing on Monday morning and we can discuss the details?"

"Sure, Mr. Lewellyn." There was no doubt in my mind what the *special project* would entail and I shifted uncomfortably in my chair as I tried to adjust my growing hard-on.

"Very good." He told my dad and brothers how nice it was to meet them, told me that he looked forward to our Monday meeting, and then the three men left the restaurant.

My dad was super excited that I had garnered the attention of the factory manager and speculated for the rest of the night about what the special project could be that Mr. Lewellyn had wanted to meet with me about. None of his guesses involved Mr. Lewelyn fucking me, which was what I certainly thought it would be. I let my dad wallow in his ignorance, realizing that denial was probably a pretty good coping mechanism for him.

I was excited all day Sunday waiting to have the conversation with Mr. Lewellyn. Choosing not to mention it to Marcus until after I knew for sure what the boss wanted, I spent the day playing cards with my family and watching baseball on TV.

Monday morning came in a rush as I decided what to wear and caused myself to run a little bit behind. I was only a few minutes late when I got in the elevator at IBM and pressed the button for the top floor. The doors opened onto a reception desk flanked by two huge ferns. The receptionist looked up at me in annoyance and didn't say a word.

"I'm supposed to see Mr. Lewellyn today," I said, my voice sounding awkward and unsure.

"He's waiting," he snapped. "Last door at the end of the

hall." He pointed with military precision.

"Thanks," I said, feeling even more pressure.

Making my way down the hallway, I found the last door and saw the impressive brass plaque beside it with Mr. Lewellyn's name and title on it. I knocked and then tried the knob. The door was unlocked so I pushed it open.

Mr. Lewellyn was seated behind a heavy wooden desk that was piled high with reports and coffee mugs. Not the kind of desk I expected him to have. He looked up when I walked towards him and said, "Ah, Loch. Come have a seat."

"Sorry I'm late," I said, almost under my breath as I sat down in a large fabric armchair.

"You won't be late again," he said firmly as he closed the report he was looking at and stood up from his chair.

"Yes, sir," I said as a way to let him know that I understood. Mr. Lewellyn was a stone cold dominant, of that I was sure.

He stood in front of me, leaned against his heavy desk, crossed his legs at the ankle and said, "So, Loch, I have a proposition for you."

I bet you do.

"I would like to promote you and make you my administrative assistant."

Is my desk located under yours?

Mr. Lewellyn's beady eyes were constantly scanning me while he talked. "I have need of your special talents and am willing to make it worth your time."

Setting my jaw for a negotiation, I asked, "And what would your proposition entail, Mr. Lewellyn?"

"Right down to business, huh?" he asked. "Very well. I would like to have one night a week where I can fuck you at my leisure and each weekend, of course."

There was absolutely no passion in his voice. This was a business transaction with almost no emotional attachment to it at all. It was probably the exact arrangement that I needed.

"Are you considering my proposal?" he asked when I

stayed quiet for a while.

"I have some terms of my own," I said to him.

"Of course. Let me hear them."

"If I accept your proposition, there will be no promotion and I will keep my job on the assembly line."

Mr. Lewellyn looked at me oddly and tilted his bald head to the side before saying, "Okay."

I continued, "In addition, you will not show me any special attention at work or even acknowledge my presence."

"I'm pretty good at that, am I not?" He smirked.

"You are," I agreed, chuckling.

"So, it's a deal?"

"Not yet." I was in control in this negotiation, and I was not ready to relinquish that control yet. "Do you have a contract with a Servant presently?"

"I do."

"And he cannot satisfy you?"

"He does, but it is always nice to have something different on the side," Mr. Lewellyn admitted.

This statement let me know everything I needed to know about the man. Mr. Lewellyn was a true cocksman. He loved having sex more than any other hobby he had and he was willing to pay for the privilege.

"And what type of sex would it be?" I asked flatly.

"What?" he asked, probably caught off-guard by my directness.

"What's your fetish?"

"Bondage. I would like to tie you up," he replied, mirroring my directness. "It will never lead to physical pain or trauma."

"Let me see your cock." I could see the substantial bulge in his dress pants twitch occasionally as he was titillated by our discussion.

"Excuse me?"

"Show me your cock. I have to make sure that I will reap

some enjoyment from this as well."

My boss seemed to see the sense in what I was saying. Unzipping his dress pants, Mr. Lewellyn reached inside his fly and pulled a monster of a fishing rod out of the opening. "Can you work with this?" He smirked, already knowing the answer.

"Nice prick," I said, still studying it. It was not as thick as Marcus' but just as long. It was a pale pink color with a small, mushroom-shaped, dark purple head.

"Thanks, I'm pretty proud of it," he said as he stuffed it back into his pants and zipped up. "That pretty much seal the deal for you?"

"Mr. Lewellyn, if you think I am considering your offer because of the size of your cock, you are mistaken. My boyfriend back at school gives me everything I need in that department."

"Marcus Battle?" he asked.

Shocked that he would know that name, I answered, "Yes."

Seeing that his direct hit wasn't going to have the effect he had intended it to have, he acquiesced. "Of course. I stand corrected."

"I will accept your proposal with a few provisions. I will be yours each Wednesday after the gym and one day on the weekend except for one weekend a month, when you can have me for the whole weekend."

"Very well. And what can I do for you, since you have refused my promotion?"

"Does IBM have a scholarship?"

"They do."

"I would like to win that scholarship for the next three years to help my dad out with my tuition for school. And if I so choose, I would like a standing job invitation waiting on me here, for the summers and after college."

"Deal."

"I'll expect the proposal in writing before our date on Wednesday."

Mr. Lewellyn looked at me with a look of respect on his face. "That can be arranged. Man, I didn't know what to expect of you, but I don't think this negotiation was it. You are one hell of a negotiator, Loch."

I smiled for the first time. "Pleasure doing business with you, Mr. Lewellyn." I stood and held my hand out to him, shaking his.

"My pleasure."

"It will be," I said smartly as I headed for the door letting him take in the view of my ass all the way across the room.

CHAPTER FIVE

The boys on the line were very curious about why I was late coming to work, but I told them that I would tell them all about it over lunch. Our manager, Phil, was filling in for me at my station when I arrived and then he lingered to hear the gossip. I didn't want this to get out to middle management, so I kept tightlipped about what happened until lunchtime.

My buddies on the assembly line and I went out to lunch at a nearby Wendy's so we wouldn't be as easily overheard. I told them about Mr. Lewellyn's proposal, leaving out the specific days and his fetish, of course. They were not surprised that he wanted to fuck me, but were surprised that I turned down the promotion and easier job.

"What? And leave you jackasses to build those machines without me?" I asked, ribbing them as we headed back to work. I had made sure that they knew that I did not want any of this information to get out.

After work, I knew that I was going to have to tell Marcus about the meeting and the plan. I was not really looking forward to it, even though it was what he wanted me to do. My thoughts were that he would like Mr. Lewellyn's age, the fact that he was well-off and in a position of power, the contract that I asked for, and the limits that I set on him. I did not think he would like the bondage aspect of it at all.

There was a level of trust needed to engage in bondage and I was willing to bet that Marcus would never trust someone to do this with me except for himself. I worked the rest of the day on the assembly line trying to construct my side of the conversation with Marcus while I tried to anticipate his every reaction and question.

I was pretty tired when I finally got into my car and headed home. I wanted to call Marcus and get the conversation out of the way, but at the same time, I wanted to fully concentrate on it, so driving and talking was not the best idea. Once in my bedroom at home with the door closed, I pressed his name in my list of favorites and lay down on my little twin bed as his phone rang.

"Hey," Marcus answered cheerfully. "You just leave work?"

"Just got home. You?"

"Same. It started to rain, so Dad let us go early. Weren't you supposed to go to the gym today?"

Marcus always knew when I was avoiding something or not doing what he wanted me to do. "I was, but I needed to talk to you first."

His tone changed immediately. "What's wrong?"

"I got called into the big boss's office this morning."

"Oh?" I could tell by Marcus' tone, even on that one little word, that he already saw where this was heading.

"Yeah. Apparently, he has been watching me and checking up on us."

"Us?" Marcus asked in surprise.

"Yeah. He knew all about you."

"What did he want?" Catching himself, he added, "I mean, I know what he wants, but what did he say?"

"He wanted to make a deal with me," I said gingerly, wrinkling my face against his probable bad reaction.

"He wants to fuck you," Marcus said levelly.

I answered carefully, "Yes."

"Doesn't he have a Servant?"

"He does, but says he wants another one on the side."

"Ass hound," Marcus said, summarizing.

"Apparently."

"Did you agree to it?"

"I asked a bunch of questions, set some rules, determined what I might get out of it, demanded it all in writing, and then I did agree to it."

"Good. Tell me all about it and him." I could hear that Marcus had steeled himself to the idea that some other man was going to be laying claim to his piece of ass. It was probably tearing him up inside, but he was not going to show me that side of him.

I updated him on all the details. He was extremely happy with Mr. Lewellyn's age, the fact that I didn't think he was that attractive, and my negotiation skills, but had concerns over the bondage aspect, like I thought he would. We talked about all of the possible scenarios and what I would do to protect myself each time.

"Can't I just come to Ohio and be with you? I could work for your father and you could fuck me all night every night so that I stay on an even keel," I pleaded with him.

"That sounds like heaven, but your family would miss you and I need to concentrate on working out and practicing to make the starting squad of the team for next year."

There was silence on the phone as I kept quiet, not wanting to show my disappointment.

He continued, "You know I want what you want, don't you?"

"Yes," I conceded.

"I would do anything for that. Don't be angry or upset with me, Loch."

"I'm not."

"Good. I can't wait until I see you in July and I get to remind you that old Mr. Lewellyn has nothing on me."

"That won't be hard," I said with a snort.

"But I will be!" he said, laughing.

"You're sure you want me to do this? Because I can wait . . ."

"I'm sure. You'll be more clear-headed and will take less risks with your safety this way." His tone of voice told me that I needed to let it go because he was firm in his decision.

"Yeah, yeah, yeah," I said in a sarcastic tone.

"Don't make me come down there and punish you," he growled.

"I wish I could."

"When's your first meeting with Lewellyn?"

"Wednesday after the gym."

"Okay. Call me on Thursday morning so I know you are okay. If it gets out of hand or you don't feel comfortable, walk out or call me and I will end it. Remember you are the one in charge," he said, empowering me to be able to fend for myself if needed.

"I'm never in charge in Chapel Hill . . ."

Marcus made a growling sound through the phone. When he spoke next, I heard the want and need in his gravelly tone. "That's because you need me to be in charge of you. You crave it and are restless until I dominate you."

"I do like it when you dominate me . . ."

"Don't get me started again. I'm going to have to go masturbate as soon as we hang up as it is."

"All right. Stay safe up there."

"You too down there."

We said our goodbyes. I felt a huge sense of relief now that Marcus knew the plan and was okay with it. I even looked forward to Wednesday and Mr. Lewellyn's huge cock being inside of me. Marcus was right, as usual. I needed a good hard fuck to help me think straight.

I told my Dad that I was going to be sleeping over at one of my buddies' houses every Wednesday for the rest of the summer and watched him eye me suspiciously. I had already lied to him about the meeting on Monday, saying that it was to let me know about this scholarship that IBM was offering. I told him that I was applying for it and that it would probably help him a lot with my tuition.

Packing an overnight bag before I grabbed a bagel and coffee on my way out of the door on Wednesday, I realized that I was more than a little excited about the day and night ahead.

Mr. Lewellyn came with a bunch of suits to observe our line that morning, but he didn't even turn his head towards me. Needless to say, the rest of the college kids on my assembly line couldn't keep their eyes off of the two of us. They were so hoping for a show and I was glad that I had insisted on the no-favoritism caveat in our agreement.

My friends were all abuzz with excitement once the suits left and wanted to know why he had not acknowledged me. I had to tell them about my demand and they thought I was foolish for not taking advantage of the man while I had him by the balls.

After work, I headed to the gym and continued to follow Burns' workout plan for me. Mr. Lewellyn appeared shortly thereafter. He was dressed in a black Under Armor tank top and red basketball shorts that showed off his tremendously developed body. I made myself *not* look at him as I completed my workout.

I showered and changed into shorts and a t-shirt before I flopped down in a comfortable chair in the lobby and waited for him. Having just started to read an article on why so many NHL players were getting the mumps this year, I looked up in surprise to see my boss standing in front of me.

"I'm glad you waited for me, Loch. Shall we leave your car here?"

I was ready for that question, having already practiced

with Marcus. "No, I would like to drive. I will follow you to your house."

"I have a hotel room for us tonight," he informed me, smiling slightly.

"Okay. I'll follow you there." *Even better for my safety to be in a hotel.*

"Very well." He turned and strode out of the doors. I gathered up my bag and followed him. He had a nice dark blue BMW sedan that I followed around the block to a Hyatt.

We both walked in the lobby with our gym bags. He didn't stop at the front desk, but instead escorted me to the elevators. Once inside, he pressed the button for the top floor.

"You use this room a lot?" I asked with a raise of my eyebrow.

"To fuck? No, never, but I do have it constantly on call for when I have to work late."

I nodded my head since I had nothing else to say on the matter.

He informed me, "We will use it every Wednesday from now on."

"Okay. It's convenient."

"Yes, it is," Mr. Lewellyn agreed as the elevator stopped. He stepped across the hallway and swiped a card in the door reader. The door opened onto a spacious living area framed by a huge bed on one side and the bathroom on the other.

"This is nice," I commented as I looked around.

"You want a drink?" Mr. Lewellyn asked, heading to the bar.

"No, I'm good." Marcus and I had already decided that until I trusted him, I should not drink anything from him.

My boss poured himself something dark over ice cubes and I removed my clothes. When my boss turned around, I was completely naked and on my knees.

"Well, well, well. Look who is eager to play," Mr. Lewellyn said, clinking the ice in his glass as he walked towards me. He rubbed the substantial bulge in the front of his dress khakis right onto my face. "I can see that we need to start slowly."

I wasn't sure what he meant by that, so I watched him carefully as he walked away from me. He hefted his gym bag up onto the couch and unzipped it. Pulling something black from the bag, he came back over to me and showed me the silken cords that he had grasped between his hands.

Mr. Lewellyn's eyes were alight with desire as he rubbed the soft braided cords against my cheeks. He extended them and let them brush my cock and balls before moving around behind me and letting the cords tickle my ass cheeks.

Suddenly, he dropped to his knees and bound my wrists together with the soft cording. It didn't hurt, but he tied me securely. There was not a single chance of escaping the knot he tied. Telling myself to take a deep breath, I forced myself to relax.

Mr. Lewellyn moved around me, paused directly in front of me, spread his legs, unzipped his fly, and pulled his raging boner out of the opening. "Is this what you want, Loch?"

"Yes," I answered plainly.

"Yes, Sir," he admonished me.

"You're not my Master, Mr. Lewellyn," I said defiantly.

He smirked at me and his beady eyes glittered with delight. "I am your Master for the next twelve hours, Loch. Now, let me hear it."

"Yes, Sir."

"Ah, now that sounds perfect," Mr. Lewellyn gloated. "I should give you this now, Loch," he said, grabbing his big joint. "But I'm not quite ready to let you have it yet." He walked over to his bag and pulled something else out. Walking back over to me, he let the black silky material he was holding touch my face.

He asked, "Do you see this blindfold?"

"Yes. Sir," I said, almost forgetting the title.

"I would love to blindfold you, so that you couldn't see what was coming. You wouldn't be able to anticipate your next move or mine, Loch," he said as he continued to lightly stroke my skin with the blindfold. "But, you are new, so I will give you a chance. I will ask you a series of questions and if you answer honestly, then I will not use the blindfold."

"Okay."

Mr. Lewellyn made a face like he had just eaten something unpleasant. "Did you tell the boys on your line about my proposition?"

"Some of them," I answered honestly.

"Why would you do that?" he asked.

"Safety," I answered immediately. He couldn't fault me for that and I would never apologize for that.

"Explain."

I hesitated, but decided to not pull any punches. "If the boys knew where I would be every Wednesday night and on the weekends, then you would be less likely to do something crazy to me." I had to look away from his eyes.

"You think I'm crazy?" Mr. Lewellyn asked, sounding a touch hurt.

I looked back into my boss's eyes. "No. But, I don't know you well enough to really decide yet and I have to protect myself."

He seemed to believe that I was telling the truth. "Understood. Did you tell your family also?"

"No, Sir."

"Why not?" he asked in shock.

I had to think for a second about that. "I didn't want my dad to be disappointed in me."

"You think he would be disappointed in our arrangement?"

I felt my neck and ears start to get hot. "I think he would be disappointed in me as a person for agreeing to it."

"I understand. Personally, I thought the way you handled that negotiation with me was magnificent. I think your father would be super-proud of a son that could do that."

"Thank you, sir."

Mr. Lewellyn looked down at me with a look of respect on his face. "I would be very proud of my boy if he handled himself like that."

I nodded and said, "Maybe, but then, would your boy be kneeling in a hotel room, naked, with his hands bound behind him, in front of an almost complete stranger who has his cock out. Would your boy soon be sucking that huge cock down into his throat and writhing under the stranger as he gets thoroughly fucked by him. Would you still be proud?"

Mr. Lewellyn's cock throbbed and bounced at my words. "I see your point," he said dryly. "You are unlike any Servant I have ever met before, Loch."

"I am not a Servant," I said as I interrupted him.

"Pardon me," Mr. Lewellyn said. "You are the most unusual marked man that I have ever met."

"Thank you."

Mr. Lewellyn continued just as if I had not interrupted him at every turn. "You're smart and confident, Loch. You are able to push emotions out of the way and make informed smart decisions for your future. You don't cowl to authority or try to manipulate your position." When I didn't respond, he said, "It is quite refreshing."

"I'm glad that I could entertain you," I said with a slight smile.

"Oh, you're going to do more than just entertain me," he growled as he stepped towards me, his big cock swinging low between his muscled legs.

CHAPTER SIX

My first fuck session with my boss was in full swing. Mr. Lewellyn had immediately bound my arms behind my back, but instead of fucking me right away, he had chosen to talk instead. I was thrown off by his approach, but at the end of our talk I found myself to be oddly turned on.

"I guess we will put away this blindfold for now and save it for another day," my boss said as he tossed the black piece of fabric towards his gym bag.

Stepping towards my face, Mr. Lewellyn fed me his cock and I used my tongue and lips to try to satisfy him. It was weird not to have the use of my hands. I never realized until that moment how many things I usually used them for when giving a blowjob.

"Good mouth," he commented, almost to himself.

Mr. L's thick cock tasted fresh and clean so I sucked it until he pulled it out of my hungry hole. He dropped his gym bag to the ground, helped me up onto the bed, and forced me down onto my stomach. He untied my hands, only to retie them to the bedposts.

"I've been looking forward to this for a while now," my boss commented as he lubed his cock with one hand and ran the other lightly over my outstretched back and upturned ass cheeks.

I was used to Marcus and me not talking while we fucked and I could already tell that Mr. Lewellyn was a talker. He commented on each part of the fuck, as if he was a play-by-play announcer at one of Marcus' football games. I decided to keep quiet except for grunts and groans to let him know I was still there.

"Going to fuck you hard now, Loch," Mr. Lewellyn informed me as he climbed up onto the bed and straddled my legs.

"So fucking tight," the big boss said as he worked two lubed fingers into my dark chute. "I thought you and young Mr. Battle were fucking like rabbits while you were at school?"

"We were." I had wanted to stay quiet, but I couldn't help but correct him.

"Then your ass sure has missed him. It has shrunk so tight that I'm not sure you will be able to take me," he said, breathing heavily.

"I can take you with no problem, don't you worry."

"You're so fucking confident. I love that about you! We'll just have to see if you can back up that confidence, won't we?" he asked as he pushed his velvety soft cock head between my ass cheeks and parted my anal ring.

I moaned at the familiar feeling of exquisite painful pleasure that he was producing in me. Immediately missing Marcus, I made myself stay in the moment and blew out air to try to relax in order to do so.

"Oh, that's it." Mr. Lewellyn moaned above me as I squeezed his cock with my ass as he slowly pushed it inside of me. Inch by inch he slid it further inside, stopping before he hit the bottom.

"Keep going. Give it all to me," I encouraged him.

"You can't take it all. No one ever has the first time."

"I'm not your typical marked man, Mr. Lewellyn," I said confidently. I had taken Marcus Battle on his first try and he was bigger, so I knew that I could take Mr. L's joint.

"I'm beginning to see that," he said with excitement in his voice. He angled his body over my backside and with one hard thrust sent the rest of his big cock into my anal channel.

"Fuck me!" he said in delight.

I jerked against the silken cords that bound my wrists, trying to avoid the rock-hard cock that was impaling me and at the same time, trying to get even more of it inside me. But my boss was buried up to the nuts in me and there was no more cock to give. His well-trimmed pubic hair was tickling my ass cheeks.

Mr. Lewellyn started to fuck and the rest of the night blurred into one bound fuck after another. My new boss knew his way around a marked guy's body and he certainly knew how to fuck. He was a master of domination and I learned a lot from him that night. He varied his speeds just to keep me off kilter, sometimes not even fucking at all, but holding his hard cock inside me and softly teasing my skin somewhere other than my ass.

Mr. L fucked me while I was tied in an X shape at the corners of the bed, he fucked me while I stood with my wrists and ankles tied together, dipping his dick down into me like a oil well, and he fucked me standing against a mirror while my hands were bound to the small of my back. My face was pressed against the smooth cool glass of the mirror as he destroyed me from behind.

Throughout our session, he talked constantly, complimenting me and telling me how much he was enjoying himself. I could tell that Mr. Lewellyn was pretty vain about his body and especially his cock, but he recognized true talent in me, or so he said.

I was happy that this sex didn't have an emotional component to it. That might have tempted me from what I had with Marcus, but this was just an arrangement so it didn't even compare with what I had with my boyfriend. This was a cold business dealing, pleasurable and satisfying for me, but still nothing more than getting my rocks off by being fucked thoroughly.

When Mr. Lewellyn was spent and he untied me, I went to soak in a very hot bath. My boss had pretty good stamina for someone his age, but he couldn't keep it up all day and night like Marcus, who had completely spoiled me.

I watched Mr. Lewellyn's finely chiseled body as he stepped into the shower and cleaned the sex off. He was an amazing example of what a body could be if kept in the proper working order for years.

We both dried off and went to the bed. I decided to watch some TV from the bed while he curled up and fell asleep. Overall, it had been a very good night with my new boss and I knew that our relationship was going to work out nicely.

I texted Marcus from my cell phone the second Mr. Lewellyn fell asleep and let him know that I was okay.

I'm glad you're okay

I am

I was a nervous wreck waiting to hear

It wasn't bad, pretty vanilla actually

I'll get the deets tomorrow, but have to know now . . . is he better than me?

Fuck, no!!

LOL

I miss that big stick of yours like crazy . . . and you too, of course!

Ditto . . . well, not your stick!

Haha! Goodnight

Talk to you tomorrow

The next morning, Mr. Lewellyn woke me by lifting my leg and pushing his morning wood into my sore hole. I was lying on my side facing away from him, so he slowly worked that hard piece of meat inside of me.

"I dreamed about being inside of you all night," he whispered into the back of my head.

"Sometimes dreams do come true," I said with a chuckle as

he pushed more of his breakfast sausage inside of me.

"They certainly do," he said as he wrapped one of his bondage cords over my wrist. I held my other arm up to him so that he could bind that wrist as well. He pulled my arms back and put his head through the hole made by my arms. "I know I had a prayer answered when you walked onto my factory floor, Loch."

I held my breath. I didn't want this to become anything more than it already was. Fortunately, Mr. Lewellyn didn't say anything else as he hooked my leg behind his ass and wrapped his big arms around my torso. He fucked me hard and fast from the side and then we showered together without another word.

Mr. L had ordered a breakfast for two sent to our room and we talked about his upcoming day while we ate. We also made plans for the weekend. He wanted to take me to his hunting lodge outside of Beaufort for the weekend if I accepted it as our one long weekend that month. I agreed to his plans and soon we departed for work in our separate cars.

The boys on the line gave me shit about standing up at my workplace that day. They knew the reason why I couldn't sit and made sure that I was well aware that they knew. I laughed at their crude jokes and encouraged them even more by making snide comments myself. I really enjoyed working with these guys and was glad that I hadn't left the line like Mr. Lewellyn had offered.

I talked to Marcus all the way home from work that day and he was glad that I had liked the session with Mr. Lewellyn, but even happier that I was not enamored with him. I admitted that he was probably right that I needed the cobwebs cleaned out of my ass every so often to settle me down and I told him that I wished that it was his broom that could have done it.

Marcus replied that he would make sure no cobwebs developed as soon as we were back at school and we hung up on a happy note just as I pulled into the driveway of my house. I went straight to my bedroom, put on board shorts and climbed into my dad's hot tub.

I spent the rest of the week doing laundry and packing a small bag for my weekend away to Mr. Lewellyn's hunting lodge. I told my family that I was going fishing with some buddies from school near Savannah and my dad gave me some money for bait.

I was pretty sure that I was the bait, but I kept my mouth closed about that!

CHAPTER SEVEN

That Friday, I left my overnight bag in my car, worked my shift, and waited for Mr. Lewellyn to come out to the parking lot to meet me. Most of the cars from my shift were gone and the few workers that were on the night shift had already reported to work, so when my boss joined me at my car, we were virtually unseen.

"You ready?" he asked with a sly smile.

"Ready," I said, feeling excitement and tension at the same time.

Mr. Lewellyn looked at me curiously and asked, "Will you let me drive us?"

"Sure," I said flippantly.

"Oh, you trust me now?" He smirked.

"I think so," I said with a laugh as I got out of the car with my bag.

Mr. Lewellyn looked down at my bag with curiosity and then he shook it off. "I'm over here in the Range Rover," he said, pointing to a prime parking space at the front of the lot. "Your car will be safe here over the weekend."

I followed him to his SUV and climbed into the passenger seat after throwing my bag into the back seat. We were headed out of town before Mr. Lewellyn spoke again.

"I've not been able to get you out of my mind the past few days, Loch."

Not what I wanted to hear. I turned to look at him. If he was going to get emotionally involved, I was going to have to pull the plug on this business transaction.

He backtracked when he saw my frown. "It probably was because it was exciting to have two options to fuck and because it was all so new with you." He cautiously continued while he watched the road in front of him, "I kind of took it easy on you in the hotel. I plan on correcting that this weekend."

"What does that mean?" I asked before I could stop myself.

He turned to look at me and said, "I would like to have you bound for most of the weekend."

Chuckling, I said, "Doesn't sound like much fun for me."

"Oh, I'll make it fun for you, don't worry."

"You gonna prod me with your funstick?" I asked, laughing.

"I am . . . along with other things," he said, grinning like a fool.

I laughed at his childlike demeanor and turned back to looking out of the window. I was glad that Mr. Lewellyn was relaxing a bit and I couldn't wait to see what he had planned for me.

It didn't take long for us to reach the hunting lodge, if that was what it was called. It was a beautiful log cabin that was huge with at least three stories.

"Really cool!" I told my boss.

"I'm glad you like it, Loch. Grab your bag and follow me," he ordered.

I followed Mr. Lewellyn onto the porch where he unlocked several deadbolts on the front door before stepping inside.

"Look around while I turn on the air and hot water heater. I'm going to want to tie you up when I finish so this might be your only chance to see the house," he informed me with a shit-eating grin.

I took Mr. L's advice and looked everywhere. There were five bedrooms and the same number of bathrooms. Everything was first class and I wondered just for a second if this is the kind of place that I could have expected to live in if I had entered The Service and become a Servant to some rich old dude like Mr. Lewellyn.

"Beer?" my fake Master asked, coming up into the main room from the basement.

"Sure."

Mr. Lewellyn grabbed two bottles of beer out of the fridge and handed me one. We talked about the house for a little while as we drank our beers and then he asked me if I was ready.

I nodded and he led me to the master bedroom. It looked like any other bedroom in a vacation house, except on closer examination, there were small metal circles embedded in the walls in different places. These were cleverly disguised by the wallpaper on the walls.

"Strip, Loch," he commanded.

I did as ordered and watched as Mr. Lewellyn opened a dresser drawer and pulled out several things. The first one was a blindfold just like the one he had shown me on Wednesday. He didn't talk about what he wanted to do, but instead wasted no time in putting the blindfold on me.

It was a weird feeling not knowing what was coming next, but apparently Mr. Lewellyn only wanted to tie me up for now. He made sure that I was comfortable, even though I was spread-eagled on my back on the bed and tied securely in place.

"I've got to go take care of something," he informed me, right before putting a set of headphones on my head. Music was pouring into my ears from them. I liked the new U2 album, but wanted to be able to hear what was going on around me. Now, he had robbed me of three of my senses. I had to admit that Mr. Lewellyn had me intrigued.

I listened to try to hear Mr. Lewellyn leaving the room, but could not. He must have been gone for quite a while, because

I drifted off as the excitement of the moment passed and the adrenaline left my system. I woke with a jerk as I realized that someone had sat down on the bed beside me.

Mr. Lewellyn was untying my legs and arms. He worked each one of them back and forth before moving onto the next one. I was loose now, but still unable to see or hear. I felt his hands on my thigh and then a strange feeling of a strap being placed around it. Pulling my hand down to him, Mr. L attached another strap around my wrist.

Soon, I was strapped with my wrists right beside my thighs, bending me in half like a turtle on its back. I felt my boss' weight on the bed near my head and instinctively opened my mouth. He easily slid his long thick cock between my lips and down to the back of my mouth.

I tried to twist onto my side to make it easier to blow him, but my boss kept me restrained on my back by holding me down with a hand in the middle of my chest. Sucking his cock like a baby bird being fed a fat spring worm, I did the best I could, given the situation.

Mr. Lewellyn got hard in a hurry and soon pulled his dipstick out of my hungry hole. He pulled the headphones off of my head and moved down to the end of the bed, pulling me to the edge with him.

"Loch, I wanted you to know that Wednesday was something special. Not because you were the perfect sub, because you weren't, but because you are the most unusual marked man that I have ever met. Your story is so unique and you are one of the most confident men that I have ever met."

What's this leading to?

"And when I fucked you, it was amazing. I couldn't keep it to myself, so I told my brother about you. He has always been my confidant and I his, so I knew he would be intrigued by you as well."

Did he bring his brother along? Is that where this is headed?

Mr. Lewellyn placed the head of his big cock against my

small puckered hole as he continued, "Richard was intrigued and thought you might be open to his lifestyle as well."

His lifestyle? What the fuck is he talking about?

"You see, Loch, when I made it big and called for my first Servant, I wanted to also spend my money on a Servant for my brother, who had always been my best friend. But it turned out that he didn't really need one."

Without any warning, Mr. Lewellyn moved his hips forward and sank his monster cock inside of me. My anal ring flew open and then squeezed his shaft as he penetrated me. I arched my back and a jagged groan came out of my mouth as he pushed all the way to the nuts into me.

"You feel that?" he asked. "That feeling of being totally invaded by a hot cock? Well, it turns out that my brother, Richard . . ." The blindfold was snatched off of my face. I blinked my eyes to adjust them.

I could see someone was lying on the bed beside me and when he came into focus, I saw that it was Richard. He was lying in the same position that I was in with the same restraints on his wrists and thighs.

"It turns out that Richard loves that feeling as much as you do, Loch," Mr. Lewellyn finished.

I watched in fascination as a stranger entered the room, a big hard cock swinging between his legs. He stepped right up to the bed beside us and pointed his dick as Richard's asshole.

My boss' big hummer was throbbing away inside my ass as we watched the scene unfold in front of us.

Richard's voice broke the silence. "Give it to me. Give it all to me, Bill."

Bill didn't hesitate any longer. He pushed his hips forward, sending his cock blazing into Richard's ass until he hit the bottom. He was a big thick man who looked like he fit right in here in the woods, with a hairy beer belly and random tattoos all over, including two full matching sleeves. His dark, rust-colored beard was speckled with white hair and I was pretty sure that he was bald under his camo baseball cap.

"That's where you need to be," Richard sighed as he closed his eyes and laid his head back onto the mattress.

Mr. Lewellyn began to thrust back and forth into me while he told me the story. "Our father used to bring us here to camp and hunt when we were boys. Bill was the son of the guy who owned the land. Richard, Bill, and I would stay up late, swim naked, and fool around together. Bill and Richard took it to another level and began fucking shortly before they told me about it. . I wasn't thrilled about it at first, because I thought my brother was being taken advantage of, even if he said that it was what he wanted. But they were adults and Richard could decide for himself what he wanted and he chose Bill. I bought the land from Bill's old man ten years ago and built the house. So, the two of them are very happy with each other and the three of us have gotten along famously."

Bill nodded his head in my direction and said, "Pleasure to meet you." His hips never once stopped thrusting his fat cock into Richard's hole.

Mr. Lewellyn was fucking me so deep and fast as he told the story that he was becoming breathy and a sheen of sweat appeared in the middle of his chiseled chest. Bill was fucking Richard just as hard and Mr. L's brother was moaning like crazy beside me.

Richard was not marked, so that meant that he was sexually attracted to women, like every other NOMAR in our world. But, he had a fetish for being fucked in the ass. It was not unheard of in our world. In fact, there were quite a few NOMARs who found work in Service Stations—those brothels for men without Servants where they could get their rocks off.

I assumed that Richard and his brother were worried that I might find this whole thing offensive but who was I to judge. I personally didn't have a problem with it at all. I did wonder if maybe Richard had been abused as a child. I decided that I would ask Mr. Lewellyn later.

Mr. Lewellyn finally slammed into me so hard that it would have propelled me backwards on the bed if I had not been secured as he pumped a load of hot cum into my hot hole.

"Fuuuucccckkkkk!" he groaned with his head back and his eyes closed.

His brother grunted, "Fill me up with scalding hot spunk, Bill."

"Yeah," Bill replied. I guessed he was a man of few words.

Mr. Lewellyn collapsed on top of me, panting hard. When he finally got his breath back, he asked me, "What do you think, Loch?"

"I think I might want to take my turn at Richard to see which Lewellyn brother is better." I smirked.

"Now that's what I'm fucking talking about!" Mr. Lewellyn said with excitement. He was grinning when he turned to his brother for confirmation.

"Let's do it!" Richard said. "Okay with you, Bill?"

"I'm going to get another beer. I'll want to fuck a hole when I come back, so you guys figure it out."

"Never know what you're gonna find in these woods," I said dryly.

"Get used to it," my boss said, laughing as he pulled out of me and began to untie me. "We Lewllyns ride hard and fast.".

CHAPTER EIGHT

After being released from my restraints, I sucked Richard and his brother back up to a hardened state again. Fortunately for me, Richard only liked getting fucked and did not really do anything else with men except for that.

I gave Richard a hard fuck while my boss approached me from behind. I was amazed when Mr. Lewellyn pushed me forward and plowed me with his big dick. I had been the middle of the sandwich on a couple of occasions before and I had a difficult time staying hard, but this time I concentrated and was able to pull it off.

It had been a really long time since I had fucked anyone and I had to admit that Richard's sloppy ass felt good even though it was loose from years of Bill's fat cock penetrating it. Richard seemed to like it and was vocally complementary towards me during his ride.

I spent the rest of the weekend tied in different rooms in different configurations, constantly being fucked by one man or another or blowing whoever stepped up to my mouth. Richard tried fucking me and seemed to enjoy it as much as his brother, so I was kept very busy. I couldn't get a good read on Bill, but his fat cock stretched me out as he came with gusto each time he fucked me.

The only time I was released from my restraints was to go out to dinner at night, and afterwards to sit by the fire and talk. One night we had a very frank discussion about Bill and Richard and I was pleased to learn that Richard had been the one to initiate the contact with his friend after years of feeling badly about himself. He told me that he has never felt depressed since releasing his secret and having the attention of his long-time friend. Bill was one of the luckiest NOMARs ever—having a Servant for life.

Sunday night, Mr. Lewellyn took me back to my car and I called Marcus to let him know that I was okay. He asked me how it was and I flirtatiously told him that I learned a few things that I couldn't wait to show him.

Marcus seemed intrigued, but I could hear that some kind of distance was developing between us and I didn't like it at all. I reminded him that my family was coming up to vacation and to see him in two weekends and he seemed to perk up a bit.

Maybe it was just too much to ask him to go without sex for three months and then have to listen to my stories of other guys fucking me. I would have to dial it back from now on when I talked with him. The last thing I wanted was to cause him pain or to affect our relationship in any way.

I spent the next two weeks focused on Marcus. I sent him funny cards, frequent texts and photos of cool stuff that I saw, and any mention of him or the team in the press. My onslaught of positive interaction with him seemed to help as I could literally hear him come out of the funk he had been in for the last few weeks.

My brothers were so excited to go to one of the greatest amusement parks in the world and mistakenly read my excitement the same way. They had no idea that I considered Marcus Battle's cock and body to be my own personal amusement park and that I planned to ride him over and over again. My brothers and I excitedly searched the park's map on the internet and planned out how we could ride everything in the fastest way.

I had saved my paychecks from the summer and handed

my dad a big wad of cash in an envelope the day before we were supposed to leave.

"What's this?" Dad asked.

"It's my summer pay to help you pay for us to go on this trip," I explained with a tone that said that it should have been obvious.

"You didn't have to do that, Loch," he said with true fondness in his eyes for me.

"I know, but this trip is my idea and we're going to see my friend, so I feel a little responsible."

"Let him pay, Dad," my brother Paul said while putting mashed potatoes on his plate. We had just sat down to dinner and my brothers were apparently famished.

"He won't need to," Dad said as he put the envelope down on the table and slid it back over towards my plate.

"Why?" I asked, suddenly alert. My brothers stopped arguing and eating to listen.

My father took a deep breath and hung his head. "I'm afraid that I've got bad news, boys. We won't be able to go tomorrow."

"Why?" I asked more forcibly, standing up from my chair.

My dad looked sad and then said, "I got bad news this morning."

We were quiet while he paused.

He continued. "Your grandfather passed away this morning."

I collapsed into my chair, deflated, while my brothers both gasped.

"Grandpa Clay?" I asked, in shock.

"Yeah. My cousin called this morning. They had gone to check on him and he was still in bed, which you know is not like him."

We had been to Boca Raton to visit my grandfather many times over the years and one thing that always happened was that he woke with the sun every day.

"We have to go to Florida tomorrow," I said robotically, realizing what this news meant.

"Yes," Dad confirmed.

Finally realizing that my plans were secondary to my father losing his father, I recovered myself and said, "I'm so sorry, Dad."

"Thanks, Loch. He lived a good, full life and I don't think he had any regrets. I'm sorry that it is going to ruin our vacation."

"It's okay. This is more important."

"Well, let's eat and we can decide what we want to do about leaving tomorrow," he said with obviously fake cheerfulness.

I suddenly didn't feel like eating since I was sick to my stomach. I had put all of my eggs into one basket, that basket seeing Marcus on this vacation, and now the eggs were smashed and the basket was lying at my feet in shambles. I was wrecked. "I need to call Marcus and let him know that we are not coming."

"After dinner, Loch," my dad said, spooning lima beans onto his plate.

"I'm not hungry anymore, Dad. I'm going to go call now," I said to him as I left the table before he could say anything else.

Marcus was as devastated as I had been when I heard the news. My narcissism usually kept me from feeling worse for someone other than myself, but my heart broke for my boyfriend as I told him the news. He was appropriately sympathetic and told me to tell my father that he was sorry.

I suggested that maybe I could drive the boys up for a long weekend later in the summer, but he reminded me that he would be at football camp soon and that would lead straight into school.

"Oh yeah, will you go to Cedar Point anyway?" I asked.

"Probably not," Marcus said. "I don't want to risk getting hurt right before camp. Will you get to go to the beach some while you are in Boca?"

"Maybe." I didn't want it to sound like I was vacationing when we should have been at a funeral.

"No fooling around with those Florida boys," he warned in his husky voice that drove me insane.

"I would never! I like the ones from Ohio better."

"Good. Call me when you get settled in Florida." Marcus' tone of voice told me that the two of us were okay. I was still disappointed that I wasn't going to see him, but it helped me to know that my boyfriend and I were okay.

Marcus and I said our goodbyes and I joined my family at the dinner table. I was able to eat now that I had talked to Marcus, so my family ate and made plans for our trip south.

We were soon in the Sunshine state. Dad was in pretty good spirits for a man who had just lost his father, but I wondered if it was an act — putting on a brave face for his boys. We met with the funeral director and my grandfather's pastor. It didn't take long to plan the memorial service and funeral because my grandfather's will pretty much spelled out exactly what he wanted, down to the music to be played and the type of flowers he wanted ordered.

The funeral took three days to complete and we spent the in-between time visiting with family members who came in for it. We were staying at my grandfather's condo and between the four of us we were able to get it cleaned up pretty quickly. We boxed up everything that Dad wanted to take back to Charleston and threw everything else away.

On the fourth day in Florida, I told Dad that I was going to take the boys to the beach while he just enjoyed his day. He seemed grateful and looked really tired, so I packed up the boys and drove them to the beach.

Paul and Chester wore me out, playing in the water and riding the waves. Finally having enough of the horseplay in the water, I left my brothers to it and went to lie out on my towel. I spent a lot of time on my phone with Marcus while I watched my brothers playing in the surf. He was happy that we had gotten a little vacation in while we were in Florida for the funeral.

I missed Marcus Battle terribly and told him that I didn't know whether I could wait until the end of summer or not. He told me that if he could, then I certainly could. I guess he had a point, but I didn't like it at all.

CHAPTER NINE

The waiting didn't get any better for me as the summer drug on. Even my Wednesdays with Mr. Lewellyn didn't hold my interest for very long. I was pretty miserable already, but when Marcus went to football camp and wasn't allowed to have his cell phone but limited hours at night, I thought I would go crazy.

Each night when my boyfriend called me he sounded more exhausted and I knew better than to keep him on the phone for very long. He needed to sleep and reserve his energy for the next day. So, I resorted to texting his buddies, Vance and Jeremy. They were under the same phone restrictions, but didn't seem to mind texting me at night.

Vance told me that Marcus was playing really well and had come into camp impressing the coaches with his new and improved body. I was excited to hear that and wondered exactly what he meant. Letting my curiosity get the best of me, I finally asked Vance what he meant, but he ignored my text. At the end of the first week of camp, Jeremy informed me that he thought both he and Marcus were going to win first string on the team for this season. I was thrilled to hear that, but knew better than to even mention it to Marcus since he was so superstitious about anything connected to the game.

I remembered that Friday was the day that the coaches provided marked men for the team to help them blow off steam, and the thought of it made me want to punch something. It didn't help that I didn't get a single text or phone call from Marcus, Jeremy or Vance until Saturday at noon.

I assumed the worst, of course. Never had I been so jealous before and it really made me question myself, namely *what the hell I was doing?* I had always been the one in charge in all of my relationships until now. Feeling totally out-of-control and jealous of some unknown marked man who was getting fucked by my boyfriend, I barely recognized myself.

Marcus finally called me right as I was digging through the kitchen cabinets trying to decide on what to eat. I took the phone and went to my room for privacy.

"Hey," I said as I answered him.

"Hey," Marcus' raspy voice greeted me back. Even with this one word, I could tell that he felt rested and refreshed. We were still in sync with each other enough that I could tell that much immediately.

"You okay?" I asked.

"Yeah. I got some sleep last night, so I'm feeling better."

"Did you sleep alone?" I hated myself for asking the question as soon as it was out of my mouth.

"Of course," he said, sounding irritated. "I wouldn't let you sleep with me for a long time would I, so why would I let someone else?"

Trying to do damage control, I said, "That's true, but the party was last night wasn't it?"

"Yeah, it was," he admitted.

He was purposely not being forthcoming with details, probably because of my stupid question. "Was it fun?"

"You mean, did I fuck with a lot of the marked guys?" Marcus didn't snap at me, but I could tell he was not happy with the line of this questioning.

"Well, yeah," I admitted. To me, fucking with a lot of them was far better than what I was picturing in my head of one hot marked guy setting his sights on my man and seducing him.

"What happens at camp stays at camp," he irritatingly

reminded me.

"Fuck you, Marcus!" I said angrily. It was the first words of anger that I had ever said to him.

He sighed and softly asked, "Don't you trust me, Loch?"

That made me pause. "Yes, of course, I do." The anger was out of my voice now and had been replaced by resignation.

Marcus assured me, "Then I did not do anything to break that trust, Loch."

"Okay." I took a deep breath and stopped myself. "I'm sorry, Marcus. I've never been so jealous like this before. Hell, I've never been jealous of anyone ever before. It's new to me and I'm afraid that I'm not handling it very well. I've tried to put myself in your shoes and be in the same position and try to handle it as well as you do, but I can't. I just can't, Marcus." As soon as I started, it flowed out of me like water from a bucket with a hole in it.

I heard my boyfriend's deep sigh on the other end of the phone and worried that he was done with me. Instead, he said, "Thanks for telling me that, Loch. It helps to know where your head is at and I'm flattered that you like me enough to be jealous."

Seeing that he was not going to give me any details about the party, I told myself to let it go. He had told me everything I needed to know and most importantly, he was still mine.

Marcus told me his plans for the weekend, which was pretty much lying around, letting his bruises heal, and sleeping more. My plans weren't much different, except that I had to get to the gym. When Vance told me about Marcus' new body, I had re-committed myself to working out. I wanted to make him proud of me and to keep up with him, of course.

Marcus and I ended our call on a good note and Jeremy and Vance started texting me shortly after. They told me that the party was wild and that they each got a blowjob and a fuck before they got drunk. They also told me that the marked guys at the party had heard that Marcus had a marked boy-friend and that made them swarm him. The marked boys wanted to know what Marcus had that would garner him such an honor and were determined to find out.

According to Marcus' friends, Marcus rebuffed all of the marked men's advances and they later saw him fucking one of the marked men who had not been aggressive towards him. Jeremy and Vance saw this behavior as honorable in their friend. and so did I. He was a much better person than I was, but I strived to be more like him every day.

I thanked Vance and Jeremy for keeping me included and told them to enjoy their day off. Feeling sorry for myself for being such an asshole, I sulked in my room for a while before making my way to the shower and the gym. Marcus deserved someone better than me.

The days ticked past and I felt stronger and more confident. But I had also come to a conclusion. I needed Marcus. I needed to see him, I needed to smell him, I needed to touch him, I needed to be under his weight, I needed the taste of his spunk in my mouth, and most importantly, I needed his cock inside me.

It wasn't just a wish or a desire. I actually *needed* it. Marcus was right about needing a big dick in me to keep me centered, but what he was wrong about was that it could be just any dick. He was the one that kept me even and clear-headed. He was my focus and my need.

At the end of one particularly hard work-out, everything was perfectly clear to me and I knew that I had to go to him. On Tuesday after work, I went out to the porch to talk to my father.

"Dad, I need to tell you something," I started.

"Go ahead," he said, taking a puff on his pipe.

"I'm going to go back to school on Saturday morning."

He looked at me for a minute, then said, "I thought you

might go back early."

I was shocked by his statement and asked, "Why?"

"It's the boy, isn't it?"

Swallowing hard, I answered, "Yeah."

"Marcus, is it?"

"Yes."

"I thought when our vacation got cancelled and you were unable to see him that you would leave shortly after. I was surprised that you hung around this long."

"He was busy," I admitted and we both laughed. I was surprised that my father was okay with this.

Dad stopped laughing and put on his serious face. "He's a NOMAR, isn't he, Loch?"

"Yes."

"Be careful with him, son. They can't be trusted with . . . people like you." Dad had used this tone of voice with me before when referring to the outside world in relation to me.

I looked into my father's eyes and admitted, "He's a very good man, Dad. Better than me usually. I do trust him."

"Well, that is good to hear. But, I can also hear that you've already given your heart to him, Loch," my father said with a serious face.

I shook my head and said, "No."

"Yes," he said adamantly.

"Maybe," I agreed and we laughed again. "I didn't mean to . . . it just happened, Dad."

"They say that was always the way it happened in our world when women were here with us."

"You sound like one of the professors on the History Channel," I told him with a smirk.

"I just want you to know that what you are feeling is natural, Loch. You are playing in dangerous waters, and as a man I want to tell you to run for the hills. But, as a father, I am telling you to follow your heart."

I didn't say anything to my father, but just looked at him with love and tears in my eyes. When I was able to speak again, I asked him softly, "You going to be okay without me, Dad?"

"Yeah, but I'll miss you."

"I'll miss you, too."

"Did you tell Mr. Lewellyn yet?"

Fuck! "I'm going to tell him tomorrow."

"Be good to Marcus," he threw out to me as I rose out of my chair.

"I plan to be," I said with a smile down at him.

"Not that way," he grumbled under his breath as I turned to leave him.

In every way.

I went back into the house, chastising my father for being gross.

CHAPTER TEN

Wednesday night, I broke the news to Mr. Lewellyn right before he put a hood over my head and fucked me senseless three times as I hung from a chain suspended from the ceiling. He was definitely getting his money's worth tonight.

I hung there in silence while he showered and went down to the hotel bar without me. Knowing it was part of his fantasy to have a Servant hanging in the room waiting on him, I was okay with it. I knew that the longer he stayed away, the hornier he would be. Mr. Lewellyn's stamina was unbelievable at his age, only rivaled by Marcus Battle.

I needed to ask Mr. Lewellyn for a favor and I ran through various scenarios in my head while I waited. My boss came back to the hotel room after a long time and he was with someone else. They laughed and congratulated each other as they fucked me, moved me to the bed, unzipped the mouth on my hood, and spit-roasted me. The second man didn't have much of a cock to speak of, but he made Mr. Lewellyn perform at his best so I was soon exhausted.

Finally the two men were sated and the stranger left the room, thanking Mr. Lewellyn. My boss undid my restraints and pulled the hood off of my head.

"Did you enjoy that?" he asked, obviously quite pleased with himself.

"I enjoyed you."

"Yeah, his cock wasn't much to look at, was it?"

"I didn't see it and almost didn't feel it either," I said with a chuckle.

He laughed as well and I saw my chance.

"Mr. Lewellyn, can I ask you a favor?"

"Sure, Loch."

I took a deep breath and blurted out, "Could I borrow some of your restraint equipment?"

"Want to show Marcus Battle what you have learned?"

I blushed furiously. "Yes, sir."

"What would you like?"

"Well, here is my plan. You tell me what I should use." I told him my plan for meeting Marcus at the end of football camp. Mr. Lewellyn loved a good problem and figuring out how to restrain me in an unfamiliar place was just too good to pass up.

"I'll bring you what you need tomorrow at work," he informed me.

"I'll pay for it."

"My treat. I just hope that you will come back to work for me again next summer, Loch."

"I would like that." We fell asleep and the next morning, he screwed me without any restraints. Mr. Lewellyn slow-fucked me, driving that long cock into my sore hole over and over before he finally succumbed to the milking my sphincter was giving him and exploded inside of me.

"You are something special, Loch. Don't ever sell yourself short and don't let Marcus Battle take advantage of you."

"Yes, sir." I wanted to tell him that Marcus would never do that, but it was pointless. I knew it and that was all that mattered.

Saturday morning, I packed my stuff, said goodbye to my family, and left for Chapel Hill. It was the last day of football camp and the players were finished by three, so I had seven hours to get there and get ready for my surprise.

I arrived shortly after one and ate lunch in my car, parked outside of Kenan Stadium. After eating, I turned off my car, grabbed my bag, and headed to the gate that the players used. I was hoping to see Andrew there, the security guard that knew me from last year, but instead there was an older guy manning the gate.

"Hey," I said as I approached him.

"Hey," he said warily.

"I was hoping that Andrew would be here . . ."

He interrupted me, "He's off today."

"I'm Loch . . ."

"I know who you are," he said quickly again, his eyes flicking over the bright blue mark on my face. "What are you doing here?"

His direct tone and abrupt manner put me on edge, but I decided that honesty was probably the best way to go with him. "I was hoping to surprise Battle in the locker room when he was finished with camp."

The security guard looked me up and down again and said, "I think he would like that surprise." His face broke into a broad grin that I couldn't help but to return.

"I'm sure he will," I said with a chuckle.

"What's in the bag?" he asked, suddenly serious again.

I stuttered, "Some-something that I need . . . for the surprise."

"Big bottle of lube?" he smirked.

"Something like that," I said with a smile I didn't feel.

"All right, go on and don't tell anybody that I let you in."

"I won't," I called over my shoulder as I headed down the cement passageway. My heart was racing and the thought that Marcus Battle and I were inside the same building made my cock hard as stone.

I arrived at the Carolina locker rooms, pushed open the door, and was hit with a scent that included sweat, dirt, musk, grass, piss, and cum. It was all male and intoxicating to me. It brought me right back to the start of freshman year when I had to report to the locker room and was forced to pick dates.

Stepping into the locker room, I found it to be empty and went immediately to Marcus' locker. It was not in the same place that it had been last year, but was now more central to the main room. I instantly knew it was his by the smell. I stepped up to it cautiously, grabbing some of his clothing and holding it to my nose.

Almost lightheaded with his smell in my nostrils, I knew that I had to start working on my surprise or I would be stuck here in this moment until I jacked off to his scent. I carefully unpacked my bag and began to strip my clothes off.

Mr. Lewellyn had given me several tension rods that expanded and then held between things, so I wasted no time in setting them up. Once connected, they would hold the restraints that were now around my wrists and ankles. I removed all of my clothing except for a very small jock strap that I had purchased just for the occasion and placed a bottle of lube on the top shelf of his locker. The jock completely outlined my ass but didn't cover it at all.

Running to the bathroom really quickly, I pissed and then lubed my ass as well as I could with two fingers. I washed my hands well and returned to Marcus' locker.

I unfolded two spreader bars and put them back together like a blind person's folding cane. I attached one spreader bar between my wrists and the other one between my ankles. By twisting sideways, I was able to thread each side of both spreader bars through eye hooks hanging from the two tension bars I had constructed earlier. Now I was completely restrained and helpless to turn back. There was no way I could get out of the contraption without help, so I settled in to wait.

My heart was pounding in my ears and every time I heard a random voice, I thought I might have a heart attack. Facing into Marcus' locker, I couldn't see what was happening behind me, but I could get a really good whiff of his clothes. I was a little afraid of some other player getting to the locker room first and taking advantage of me, but I thought the players would respect the rules set in place for me from last year.

Suddenly there was a rush of noise as I heard the locker room door bang open and multiple voices descend into the room. *This was happening now!*

The first group of players that came into the locker room were talking animatedly but then suddenly stopped. A weird quiet hung over the room and I wished that I could see what was happening.

Finally, a voice broke the silence. "Well, well, what do we have here?" I heard cleats move towards me and then felt a hand on my ass, so light that it made the small hairs on my skin stand at attention.

This is what I was afraid of . . .

"You know what it is, Brown."

I knew this voice!

"Stay out of it, Vance," the one named Brown said.

I could hear more voices coming into the locker room.

Vance said, "Hey Loch."

"Hey," I said softly.

Vance continued, "He is here for Battle, not for you, Brown."

"Fuck you! I wasn't gonna bother him!"

"Fuck! What is this?" some of the new guys asked as they saw past the gathering crowd around me.

"Battle is so fucking lucky!"

"I wish I came to my locker after camp and found that!"

"Yeah, we all do!"

"Here comes Battle!"

I had felt his presence even before that player had told me that he was coming. My skin tingled all over and my heart raced with anticipation.

"What's going on?" Marcus' deep voice boomed in the low-ceilinged room.

The crowd of guys must have parted because the next thing I heard was his breathy call of my name, "Loch."

He walked over to me and I could smell him — the sweaty, musky smell that I knew was his. My cock was so hard that I thought it might break through the skin of my shaft. I heard him stop right behind me and then he was touching the bars that had me spread-eagled in front of his locker. He was admiring my handiwork.

"What are you going to do, Battle?" one of the players called out to him.

"I'm going to give him what he wants," Marcus said with excitement. He wasn't a guy that got caught up in the drama of a scene, so it pleased me to no end that he sounded so excited.

There was a huge cheer from the crowd and several loud wolf whistles, as well as a few vulgar comments loudly shouted out to the room.

Marcus lowered his voice below the cheers and shouts and said to me, "This is what you want, isn't it, Loch?"

As he asked me, he slid his hand and arm between my shoulder and my face and I watched him wrap his fingers around the bottle of lube I had put on the shelf. His hand and arm were muddy and covered with sweat. Moving my cheek to the side I rubbed his arm all the way as he withdrew it. The electric charge that ran through my skin and then straight to my brain was delicious.

My mouth was so dry and my heart was beating so hard that my chest was beginning to hurt. I didn't trust myself to speak so I nodded my head ever so slightly.

CHAPTER ELEVEN

M y body rang like a bell in anticipation of Marcus' reaction to my little stunt at his locker. I heard him undress and I heard most of the other players move on to their lockers. I was grateful that most of them had the good manners not to watch Marcus and I reunite.

Hearing my boyfriend jacking his cock behind me, I could also hear some of his team mates saying things to him.

"Fuck, Battle! You should've been born black with the size of that cock of yours."

"Tear him up, Battle."

"Man, Battle is so fucking lucky!"

"Wish I had a Servant hanging in my locker!"

"Show him who the Master is, Marcus!"

I didn't care what they said. To me, there were only two people in that room — Marcus and me. And to be quite truthful, I felt like there were just two objects in the room — my ass and his cock. Nothing else mattered. Nothing else was important.

It said something about how hot Marcus was for me that he was not going to wait until the locker room cleared out to fuck me, just as my little stunt said the same thing about me.

"Ready?" Marcus whispered to me. I could hear the tremor in his voice and it affected me so profoundly that I was glad that I was suspended and unable to move.

I nodded my head in reply and tightened my grip on the chains that attached my wrist restraints to the spreader bar separating them. Lifting my ass up and back as much as I could, I felt Marcus' lower body touch mine and then Marcus' cock head was at my backdoor.

A million shooting stars ran along my neural pathways, lighting me up from the inside as he pushed that magnificent cock of his inside me. My anal ring completely spread apart as it stretched to its limit around Marcus' mighty member.

My first reaction was to lean forward to escape the brutal onslaught that was being unleashed on my ass, but the restraints stopped me from doing what my body instinctively thought it should do. My brain tried to tell my body that this was going to be one of the most hedonistic pleasures that it would ever experience, but my body was acting on pure instinct and in this case it was the survival instinct that was in the forefront.

Marcus slammed his cock inside me all the way to the short hairs. My body was pushed into the furthest limits of the restraints and my eyes flew open as he filled me up. Red flames of pain radiated out from my back side and threatened to consume me with their strength and intensity. The pain was incredible, but I loved the way he felt inside me and I loved the way I felt with him there.

"Aaaaaahhhh." The slow moan rolled out of Marcus' mouth like it was coming from deep inside of him. The same sound wanted to rip right from my insides, but my mouth was dry and my throat was raw from the tension that wracked my body.

The long thick dick inside me fit like a key handmade for my lock. It throbbed and expanded even as my sphincter squeezed and milked him. His large cock head had rammed my prostate on its way in, sending waves of pleasure flooding my senses.

Marcus laid a sweaty hand on my shoulder and the electricity radiated out from it like the epicenter of an earthquake, shaking the very fiber of my core. Then he began to fuck.

Never had I experienced a fucking like this one. Marcus pulled his big joint out of me up to the phalange of his cockhead and then drove it back inside me until his full fat balls smacked me on the ass. When he pulled back, my whole body tried to follow his movement, but the restraints held me in place. When Marcus drilled his dick inside me, the restraints held me from going the other way.

Becoming aware of a sheen of sweat developing on my skin, I realized that my body was stiff from the constant strain of the fuck. I took a deep breath between the bottom-shaking thrusts of my football player boyfriend and focused on relaxing first one muscle group and then another.

My recent sense of calm had its desired effect as I felt Marcus delve even deeper into me than he had before. My less rigid demeanor caused me to not fight the restraints and I found that I could ride the thrusts and use the restraints to flow back into Marcus.

Marcus grunted in what sounded like delight as he drilled into me over and over again. I felt hot and light-headed, but was confident that if I collapsed the restraints would hold me in place and the impalement of my ass on Marcus' cock would support me.

Thrust after thrust, my sophomore fuck buddy prodded my prostate with his massive pole and it was more than I could take. I felt my climax welling up inside my painfully full balls. The sensation of hot molten fire poured into the shaft of my cock, which twitched like it was a drumstick in the hands of Phil Collins.

I knew I was going to come without ever even touching myself, which was a fantastic feat for me, but to do so while Marcus was fucking me so deep and hard was unbelievable to me. I held my breath as my climax overwhelmed every system in my body with its urgent demand for release.

I came hard and fast, shooting long arching bands of hot

spunk directly into Marcus' locker. Only vaguely aware that I was ruining my own clothes, I continued to lurch forward with each thrust as Marcus pushed more white seed out of the end of my cock.

Marcus moaned a deep sigh of satisfaction as the muscles in my ass constricted from my climax and held his glorious shaft in its iron grip once more. He powered through it, grunting loudly each time he drilled me with his big tool.

Marcus felt so much thicker and longer inside me than he had been all of last year and even though I knew that I was imagining it, the bottom line was that Marcus' cock was still dominating me. I figured he was close to his climax because his cock felt like it had expanded two-fold since we had begun.

My boyfriend's climax came with such violence and power that the top tension bar bent slightly and one of my wrists restraints came partially un-velcroed. His whole body had conformed to mine, plastering his sweaty chest against my damp back. His crotch was completely covering my ass cheeks and he had wrapped his arms around my chest to clamp me to him.

It was an amazing display of physical dominance and even though his climax had wrecked me in the restraints, I felt perfectly safe in his arms. He held me to him as his lungs gasped for air, his piss hole opened, and he shot a huge load of man-goo inside me. Coating my anal channel with a tidal wave of spunk, Marcus' cock throbbed and bucked as it reached its release.

"Fucking hell," I whispered, overwhelmed by the moment.

"Fucking hell!" Marcus repeated, his head right beside mine inside the locker.

Slowly the world around me began to return. I could hear a few players still packing up their stuff and heading out of the locker room. I could hear the managers cleaning up the dirty practice jerseys and equipment that had carelessly been discarded all over the room. Aware of Marcus' breathing returning to normal, I could hear the small grunts of pleasure escaping his lips even as his dick continued to throb away inside of me.

"Wanna do that again, Loch?" he asked in a jagged voice.

"Will this fucking contraption hold up for another pounding like that?" I asked with a smirk.

"Do we care?"

I laughed out loud. "No, I guess we don't. Go for it, stud!"

Marcus chuckled and then began to give me a repeat performance to remind me of what I had just missed the last two months.

I didn't bother telling him and I didn't need the reminder, because I had never forgotten.

Chapter Twelve

"Fuck Battle! Maybe you ought to give the poor guy a break," one of the coaches said behind us as we hung together on the restraints recovering from the second spectacular fuck in the last half hour.

"It's good to see that he has the same focus off the field that he has on it," another coach said in passing.

"Yeah, yeah, coach. I'm going to give him a break," Marcus said as he pulled back away from me and disconnected us at the most base location from which we were joined to each other.

I was left with the most profound emptiness, but was shocked out of the sexual haze I had been fucked into.

"What if I don't want a break, coach?" I asked snarkily.

Marcus laughed and commented, "Still so hungry and so confident in yourself, Loch?"

"Did you expect me to change in two months, Marcus Battle?"

"I hoped that you would not," he answered immediately. Marcus slowly started to unhook the tension rods and unstrap the restraints holding me into place. "Where did you get this awesome set-up . . . Lewellyn?"

"Yes. Did you like it?" I held my breath as I waited for his answer.

"Couldn't you tell?"

He was so close to me that I began to get lightheaded again. The nearness of his body to me was intoxicating. His scent — sweat, cum, and his incredible musky odor, combined to overwhelm me every time I was this close. When his skin touched mine as he released me, the sparks flew just like the first time that we had fucked.

Marcus kept me facing away from him the entire time that he slowly and methodically undid every strap until every foldable rod was disassembled and back into my bag again. From the quiet around us, I assumed that we were alone.

When Marcus finally turned me around by rotating my shoulders, I came face to face with a man I didn't recognize.

"I didn't expect you to change in two months, Marcus Battle!" I repeated to him in complete awe.

"Do you like?" he asked, smiling broadly and holding his arms out by his sides.

"I love," I said, nearly drooling on him.

In the two short months that we had been away from each other, he had changed dramatically. Gone was the boyish look of the freshman that I had picked. Standing in front of me in all of his naked glory was a man. His look had totally changed and matured.

I had noticed his body, of course, but I couldn't take my eyes off of his face. His constant summer work-outs had paid big dividends. His biceps were bigger and more cut than I remembered, his stomach was smaller, and his chest was broader and more defined. His thighs looked massive to me and that caused his cock and balls to appear bigger than I remembered.

His hair had lost a lot of his youthful blond and was now a deeper copper color that looked great on him. The shaggy disorganized hairstyle was gone and he had parted his hair on the side, immediately making himself look older and more domineering. His hair hung jagged over the side of his forehead and his beard was trimmed close to his strong jaw. He was smoking hot now and I couldn't believe that he was mine!

"Wow," I said, looking at his face.

"Still like me?" he asked, like a little boy dressed up for church seeking approval.

A growl escaped my lips — guttural and primal. I had never heard anything like it before.

Marcus' eyes danced with excitement and fire. "I guess that means *yes*."

"Hell yes!" I finally was able to say. "How . . . how . . . did you do that?"

Marcus chuckled and admitted, "I worked out every time I felt horny for you."

"Good God! Did you work out day and night?"

"Absolutely! I'm taking you back to my place and gonna show how much I worked out," he threatened.

"I'm there," I said with excitement. "But I probably need to jump in the shower first."

"You and me both," Marcus said, as I noticed the dirt and grass on his magnificent body. "Let's go," he ordered as he reached past me and grabbed a shower caddy and his flip-flops. He looked down at my naked feet and said, "You'll get a raging case of athlete's foot if you walk in the showers like that."

"I don't have a choice," I said, chiding myself for not preparing for this.

Marcus solved the problem by reaching down and picking me up, cradling me in his arms. He picked me up like I was a roll of wrapping paper, even though I was six-foot-three and was not skinny by any means. He hugged me to him and bent down for me to grab the shower caddy. Marcus carried me into the shower and stood me up on a bench while he grabbed some towels and threw them onto the wet shower floor. I hopped onto them and we were soon both clean.

Marcus took a seat on the bench to wash the bottoms of his feet and when he was finished, I took advantage of his position and sat down onto his lap. I rubbed my ass against his hardening cock so that it fit in my crack like a ballpark wiener in a bun.

"Want to assume our special position?" I asked teasingly.

"Not here, Loch, not here," he replied as a modification of his regular *not today, Loch, not today* answer to my requests for sex. "That's for us and no one else."

"Yes, Sir," I teased him, once again admiring his ability to restrain himself even as I showed that I could not.

Marcus smacked my ass and said, "You need to get used to following my directives."

I stood up and turned on him. He was scorching hot already and to now be giving me commands was almost more attitude than I could handle in one day. My cock immediately got hard and slapped up against my stomach.

He looked down at it and commented, "You see, Loch. I know what you need. Your dick tells me everything. You like it when I dominate you. You love it when I command you. You desire and need me to control you."

"I do not," I tried to protest, knowing in my heart that it was true.

"Really?" he asked while smiling.

"Okay," I finally admitted, "but I don't want you to get bored with me."

"Bored?" he asked, seemingly stunned.

"Yeah. I don't want you to think that I will do whatever you say and give you no lip about it. If I did, you would just run over me and be bored in a heartbeat."

"Says who?" he challenged.

"Wouldn't you?"

"I don't think so. You've let me call the shots from the beginning pretty much and even though it's almost been a year since we started hanging out, I still am obsessed with you."

I smiled instantly. "Obsessed?" I asked with a smirk.

He blushed fiercely. "My cock is obsessed with your ass,"

he corrected.

"Just your cock. Really?" I threw his word back at him.

"Okay," he echoed me. "But I don't want you to get bored with me."

"Bored?" I asked.

"Yeah. If you know how much I think about you and how much I want to fuck you, you'll think I'm an easy target and get bored with me." He was grinning from ear to ear.

I couldn't help but grin even broader. "Says who?"

"Wouldn't you?"

"I'm even more enamored with you than I've ever been."

"Enamored?" he smirked.

"My ass is enamored with your giant cock," I corrected.

"Just your ass?" he countered.

"All of you," I finally admitted, my cock so hard that I worried that I wouldn't be able to get it to go down for quite a while.

My clothes were coated with cum, so Marcus gave me a clean t-shirt and basketball shorts to wear. I stepped into my tennis shoes and took a deep whiff of myself. I smelled just like Marcus and that did nothing at all to help me with the hard dick poking me in the stomach.

We walked to the dorm beside the stadium, Ehringhaus.

"How much longer will they let you stay here?" I asked.

"I have to go tomorrow."

"Where?"

"Coach Conrad is going to let me crash at his place until school starts back officially."

I was quiet for a minute and then I swallowed hard and asked what I had wanted to ask all summer. "Mind if I stay with you?"

He grinned from ear to ear. "I was afraid to ask you."

I laughed, relieved of all of the pressure I had been putting on the answer to that question. "Well, according to you, you could have just commanded me to do it."

Marcus chuckled and said, "I could, but that would have been too easy."

"So, I can stay?" I asked again just to make sure.

"I demand it," he answered in a condescending tone.

"If you order it, I guess I can try to make it work, Sir," I said with a shrug of my shoulders and a knowing smirk.

"Yes, try," he said with equal smirk.

CHAPTER THIRTEEN

M arcus didn't say a word as he unlocked the door to his dorm room and let me enter. One half of the room was completely barren, where I assumed his roommate had been until today. The other half of the room held Marcus' familiar bedding, clothing, and electronics. The whole room was permeated with his musky scent, and my cock was stretched to its full extent again.

He kept quiet as he closed and locked the door, approached me and gently started to strip me. Marcus Battle had never taken the opportunity to do something so intimate before. His big rough hands trembled slightly as he soon had me completely exposed to him.

Walking around me, he kept one big hand on my shoulder and with the other, grazed the fine hairs on my ass cheeks. My heart swelled with pride that this man was mine and that he was growing and maturing right in front of my eyes.

"I'm not the only one that has had a transformation," he said in a breathy half-whisper as he squeezed one of my biceps.

I raised my arms out by my side in imitation of him and asked, "You like?"

"It's awesome. I'm so proud of you, Loch."

Marcus was back in front of me, so I immediately started to undress him. His breathing changed—getting deeper and faster. I wanted to see him out of those clothes again. He was soon just as exposed as me and the two of us just stared at each other like two rams sizing each other up right before the head butt.

When he moved, it was towards the bed. He threw some clothes off of the single dorm room bed and lay down. He patted the mattress in a sign for me to join him. I walked over and sat down at the bottom and pulled one big foot into my lap. Figuring that football camp was probably a killer, I slowly started to massage his foot. Marcus' eyes fluttered shut and a deep groan rolled out of his chest.

I wanted to tell him that I would do anything for him, but I respected the silence too much to break it. Our first year together had been accented by many fuck sessions where no words were spoken. To me, it was a sign that we were constantly on the same page with each other and it was super hot. I loved him taking me without a word.

My thumbs dug into the soft meat of his foot pad and I enjoyed the Marcus smell that was released by it. Pulling each one of his big square toes, I finally couldn't resist anymore, so I bent my head down and ran my wide tongue up the center of the bottom of his foot.

Marcus sucked in a huge breath as his eyes flew open. I stared him right in the eye as I reached up and felt his big dong stretching to its hardest longest position. His cock was so hot to the touch and I could feel the blood coursing through it.

The electrical sparks flew whenever I touched him, whether it was his foot or his cock. I moved his other foot into my lap and repeated the massage again, this time lingering a little too long as I licked his foot.

Marcus growled at me and I stopped, but not without a smirky laugh. He motioned me to him with a beckoning finger, his eyes blazing with desire and need.

I squeezed some lube into my hand and stroked my footballer's big joint with it. Already having two of his massive loads inside me, I didn't think I would need it, but he seemed bigger than ever. We had established a position as our own during our freshman year together and had kept it special.

I fell into it with the ease of falling into my own bed. Standing up on the bed, I turned around facing away from him and lowered my ass down towards his crotch. Marcus had his over-sized hands on my hips guiding me down—warm and slightly moist on my skin that was chilly from the air conditioning.

Holding myself elevated right above him, I waited for him to place his beautiful cock head against my rosebud and wait, but instead I felt him punch it through.

Now, it was my time to growl. My sphincter stretched wide to allow his fat babymaker into my ass. It squeezed his hard flesh as it slid down further onto the long shaft. It felt like I was being split into two like a piece of cordwood on the chopping block.

Marcus' insistent hands continued to pull me down and down. Feeling like it was never going to end, I was soon fully impaled on his huge monster and sitting on his crotch. It was the most marvelous feeling of pleasure and pain mixed together all at once and I was completely addicted to it.

Those thick but nimble hands pulled me back onto his broad chest. Marcus' torso was heaving up and down with each breath, but his arms held tightly around my chest giving me a sense of security like no other. Pulling my legs up, I placed my feet down on his big thighs and anchored them at his knees.

Marcus' cock throbbed away inside me as he prepared for the onslaught that would be the destruction of my ass. I could do nothing but moan, lay my head back against his shoulder, and open myself to him. I wanted every inch of him inside me and I wanted to feel every bit of power he put behind each of his thrusts as he slammed deeply inside of me.

Marcus began slowly—pulling halfway out and then

slowly pumping that half back inside me. It created a slow burn in my asshole that was painfully delicious in its inception. His big cock head punched my prostate twice as often by poking it on the way in and grazing it with the phalange on the way out.

I couldn't tell you how many times Marcus Battle and I had fucked in this manner. It was his favorite and despite my reservations about it, I had come to really enjoy it as well. But, for the first time, Marcus started to roam over my body with his hands while he fucked.

It was a strange sensation and I realized that I was holding my breath and my muscles had constricted in response to it. Marcus' big hands started on my sides, gently caressing and then moving up to my armpits. His demanding hands forced my arms up above my head. His hands continued up my arms, his fingertips lightly making contact with my skin until my flesh pimpled with chills.

The more Marcus touched me the faster and deeper his cock drilled me from below. The dual sensations made me a quivering mass of nerve endings as I forced myself to relax on top of him. He was giving me everything I could have wanted and I was in heaven!

Focusing on squeezing his cock with my anal ring, I was able to produce a series of deep groans and grunts from the man whom I was lying upon. Marcus' hands continued their exploration of my body moving to my chest. He uncharacteristically pinched my nipples which were hard kernels of flesh.

My back arched and I cried out as Marcus pinched my nipples and drove his red hot poker inside me hard and fast. One of his hands clamped down on my mouth. I used my tongue to pull one of his thick digits into my mouth where I sucked it and then used it as a bit.

Marcus reached his climax, even though I wanted us to keep going forever. His fingers dug into my hips as he tried to drive deeper into me. His cock exploded inside me, coating my anal chamber with his hot sticky seed.

"Fuuuucckkk! I've missed you!" Marcus growled as his breathing returned to normal. His cock felt like it had not softened in the least as it throbbed inside me.

"I've missed you too, Marcus," I said, with a big smile on my face.

"Wanna take a nap with me and then we can go get some dinner?"

"I'd like that." I stood up and felt the dreaded empty feeling in my ass as his sloppy cock plopped out. I saw a washcloth hanging on the closet door, so I wiped Marcus and I clean before lying down on the bed with him.

"Over here," Marcus said, in his deep, commanding voice.

I smiled as I realized we were both going to sleep on the tiny twin bed. Marcus shifted onto his side against the wall and I spooned up against him. He wrapped his arms around me to hold me in place. His big body would keep me warm as I napped. I was the happiest I had ever been.

Waking up next to Marcus, I slid out of the cramped bed onto the floor feeling every bit of his four fucks in the soreness of my asshole. I kneeled in front of the bed and gave him a world class blowjob. Most men could barely dream about coming four times in the span of a few hours, but the man I had selected in that now-famous boyfriend draft could do it in his sleep.

Marcus' rod was almost always at three-quarters staff and never needed more than just the minimal prodding to be able to go and today was no different. I touched him, the sparks flew between us, and he was hard before I even got my lips around his fat cock head.

"You're going to spoil me," Marcus said with a sleepy gruff voice as his hand pushed the back of my head further onto his big shaft.

"Mmmmmmmmm," I moaned, my mouth full of Marcus meat. I had been practicing and I knew that I was able to get more of him inside me than last year. Marcus and I had mostly fucked, but Mr. Lewellyn had worked my mouth with his big joint just as much as my puckered hole.

I heard the small sounds of surprise from him as I kept going beyond my usual limit and took him down to the small hairs. His swollen cock head had entered my throat. Gripping the base of his monster, I pulled back and sucked him off in long pulling draws that soon had him whining in pleasure as he reached his climax and released his creamy man-goo directly down my throat.

"Fuck me!" he said, jerking from the sensitivity of his release. "You've gotten better at that this summer." He pulled my head off of his dick by grabbing my ears and pulling until our eyes met.

"I just wanted to reward you for the great fuck you gave me before the nap."

"Did you like it?" he smirked.

"I think we both loved it, but I wanted to let you know that your . . . increased attention did not go unnoticed."

"Ah," he said, grinning. "I didn't think you had caught that."

"I did," I said with a snort.

"I thought I might give you something new to keep you from being bored . . . with me."

I laughed out loud. "I'm not likely to get bored of you anytime soon, Marcus Battle, but I did appreciate your new additions to our fucks."

"You're welcome. Now, go shower. You stink!"

"I'm not the only one," I said, laughing. The dorm room shared a bathroom with the room beside them. I pointed at the door and Marcus nodded his head. Picking up his shower caddy that he had brought home from the stadium, I walked gingerly into the shower. My ass reminded me with each step of Marcus' sheer domination over me.

Marcus and I went to a quick dinner out and to go see *Guardians of the Galaxy*. Afterwards, we had to pack up his dorm room for the move tomorrow. That didn't take long and we were soon fucking like rabbits again.

CHAPTER FOURTEEN

"Do you think Coach Conrad is going to mind that I'm coming with you to stay for the rest of the summer?" I asked Marcus as we carried his stuff to my car.

"He might," Marcus said as he considered my question. "Do you think we might be able to warm him up to the idea?" He looked at me with a raised eyebrow.

"You want me to let him fuck me?" I asked, shocked.

He shrugged. "It wouldn't hurt."

"It wouldn't hurt? I'll hurt you, Marcus Battle," I threatened with a smile.

Marcus laughed and said, "Okay, okay. He would be unable to say no if he got some of your . . . special attention."

"We'll see if he wants to fuck around with us," I stated dismissively.

"With us?" Marcus asked.

"Yes. I don't want to be with anyone but you Marcus."

He looked concerned now. "You don't want to?"

"I don't mind letting someone join us, but I'm here for you, so I want you to always be involved. Do you mind?"

"No. That's cool," he said with a smile. "I go a little crazy when I think of you with someone else anyway."

"Want me all to yourself?"

"Always."

Coach Conrad met us in the parking lot of his apartment to help us unload. His brown eyes glinted with mischief as he saw me.

Marcus addressed him, "Coach, this is Loch."

Coach Conrad was a mountain of a man—easily six-feet-ten-inches tall with a small brown beard neatly trimmed over his square jaw. His brown eyes were constantly active below a close-shaved head of brown hair. He was in a t-shirt, flip-flops, and basketball shorts. His feet were huge, like skis and his long, lanky frame was all muscle.

"I know who Loch is," he said firmly. "I was hoping that we would get to see him before the end of the summer."

Marcus and I looked at each other knowingly.

"Do you mind if he stays with me until school starts?" Marcus asked.

"Even better," Coach said. "Absolutely he will stay with us. I used to share this apartment with the D-Line coach. You remember, him, Marcus?"

"Yeah, Coach McCreary?"

"That's him. He got another job and left last month. Luckily for you two, he was a big guy and left behind a big bed," Coach Conrad informed us as he winked at me and pushed open the apartment door with his hip.

"Lucky for us," Marcus agreed as he struggled with his clothes and crates of personal effects.

I was carrying the TV, which being the smallest guy out of the three of us, made me very proud.

"You're right in here," Conrad told us as he entered the second bedroom.

The apartment was pretty basic—two bedrooms, each with their own bathroom, that were on opposite sides of a kitchen and living room. It was on the first floor, which was nice not to have stairs. It was a typical NOMAR apartment with a weight bench in the middle of the living room, minimal decorations, a layer of dust on everything, mismatched furniture, and a pervasive smell of sweat and cum in the air.

Our bedroom was large and the king-sized bed would be perfect after that twin bed in which we had just slept in

Marcus' dorm room. Conrad gave us a tour of the apartment and I was happy to see that he was mostly a clean person and respectful of boundaries.

"Well, let's go work out," Marcus said, looking at me.

"I just carried a TV. Doesn't that count?" I asked in fake dismay.

Marcus balled up his fist and shook it at me, all while smiling. "Don't make me drag you."

"That could be fun," Conrad said, laughing as he left the room.

Marcus and I went to work out and started a pattern for the rest of the summer — wake up, eat breakfast, go for a run or swim, eat lunch, lift weights, eat dinner and fuck until we collapsed out of exhaustion.

We didn't ask Coach Conrad to join us until the second week. We had just finished off a pizza while we watched an episode of *Game of Thrones*. Conrad had started to complain that he couldn't sleep with all the fucking going on.

I looked over at Marcus, who made a very subtle nod of his head. "Maybe if you join us, you won't mind listening to it so much," I said to Conrad.

"Join you?" he asked, looking surprised.

"If you want to," Marcus said.

"With you, too?" Conrad asked Marcus.

"That's how we roll," Marcus assured him, spreading out both hands to his sides.

"You and I are not going to do anything freaky are we?" the coach asked his player with a voice filled with innocence.

"Not even in your dreams, Coach!" Marcus laughed so hard that he had to bend over to catch his breath. Coach Conrad and I both laughed at Marcus laughing so hard.

Conrad finally said, "That's cool with me. I don't want no freaky stuff, except with Loch, of course."

"I'm the freakiest one of them all," I said with a chuckle

and an elbow to the coach's ribs. I watched as his dark eyes glazed over with lust.

"When?" he asked.

I glanced at Marcus who shrugged his shoulders indifferently. Turning to our new roommate, I answered him, "When the episode is over if you want, Coach."

"I want."

Marcus and I laughed at Conrad, who obviously was very affected by just the thought of fucking around with us. He couldn't sit still during the final fifteen minutes of the show. The coach grabbed a set of dumbbells and began to do bicep curls as he sat on the couch. I made a face of disbelief to Marcus, who smiled and shrugged his shoulders again.

"Well, let's go before Conrad pops a vein or something," I finally said as I jumped up and grabbed a couple of bottles of water from the fridge on my way to the bedroom that I shared with Marcus Battle.

"Oh, he's definitely going to pop something," Marcus said, chuckling as he stripped off his tank top and basketball shorts.

Coach Conrad was naked before I could even turn around after putting the water bottles down on the nightstand. "Someone's very eager," I said, pointing at the coach's already hard cock that was pointing at the ceiling.

"Very excited to be doing this. Thanks, Marcus!"

Marcus, who was always quick to defend me, said, "Thank Loch. He's the one that is going to be doing all the work."

"I'm sorry, Loch," he said to me. "You are giving me the chance of a lifetime. No one I know has ever fucked with a marked man except Marcus here, of course. People like me don't ever dream of it. I will never make enough money to have a Servant. I will never be a Master to a marked man who hangs on my every word and action. I will never feel that rush that comes with the power or the thrill of the constant sex."

He turned to Marcus and said, "I don't know what you did

to deserve it, kid, but you better thank God for it and I hope that you are mature enough to appreciate it. Loch is a once-in-a-lifetime event, like a shooting star that you will never see again."

"Wow," I responded when I saw that he had finished.

"Amen!" Marcus said. "Now, tell him what you want him to do, Coach."

"Really?" he asked in disbelief.

"Of course. Now's your chance," I said, egging him on.

Our older roommate turned to me and said, "On your knees, boy. I want you to suck on this big donkey dick of mine!" His voice was so different from his speaking voice that I almost laughed out loud as I dropped to my knees on the Berber carpet.

Marcus looked at me sternly and I immediately squelched my smile. I guess my boyfriend wanted me to play the part of the dutiful submissive in order to give Conrad a show. I definitely could do that.

Coach walked over to me where I was kneeling with my head bowed and grabbed a handful of my blond hair. He pushed my head back and forced me to look at him. "Open," he commanded.

"Yes, Sir," I said, playing my part.

He took another step closer to me and pushed his long cock inside my mouth. He was already hard as a steel beam and leaking copious amounts of clear pre-cum. I took over and wrapped my hands around the base of his cock, which had been shaven completely bare, like his chest.

Small moaning sounds came from me as I sucked and licked his long curving shaft. I reached out and grabbed Marcus' big tool with one hand and used my fingers to manipulate him just as Conrad started to groan under the pressure.

"Holy fuck! Marcus, you gotta get in here and feel this," Conrad said excitedly.

Marcus laughed and said, "Yeah, Loch's mouth is fucking unreal, isn't it?"

"Fuck!" Conrad said, grabbing my hair again. "Get off of there or I'm going to blow right down your throat." He pulled his cock out of me and pushed my mouth onto Marcus's thick unit. "Suck your boyfriend's cock. Get him ready to fuck you," he growled.

Gladly! Coach Conrad is really living out all of his Master fantasies, I guess. I sucked on Marcus' fuck-stick and tried to get even more of it inside my mouth and throat. Gagging myself on that beautiful cock, I realized that I would experience any amount of pain or discomfort to have it inside me and I already had. That thought made me relax and the last two inches of massive meat slid down my throat.

"Fucking A, Marcus," Conrad said almost in a whisper. "Where the hell is he putting all that cock?"

"Down his sweet fucking throat now, coach!" Marcus said with more excitement in his voice than I had heard since I surprised him in the locker room after football camp.

"God damn, Marcus," the coach said in a rush of exhaled breath. "You truly are his Master."

Marcus stroked my hair with a large hand while slightly tilting my head back to make me look up at him. "Loch is an amazing man. He will do anything I ask of him and always wants to please me even at his own expense. He does all of this while still maintaining his identity and his control. If anyone here is the Master, it is Loch."

I blushed under the weight of his words and sucked his fat cock even harder to let him know that I appreciated them.

"It's hard to think of him as a Master when he's got a big fat cock in his mouth," Conrad said with all the laissez-faire of placing an order at Starbucks.

Marcus agreed, saying, "It doesn't matter whether he is inhaling a big cock or taking one up to the short hairs in his sweet ass, Loch is the shit!"

"I'm in total agreement about that," Conrad concurred. He grabbed my neck and pulled my head back off of Marcus' wang and said, "Get up on that bed, Loch. I'm going to fucking rail you out."

I scrambled to the bed and got onto all fours. Marcus grabbed the bottle of lube off of the nightstand and threw it onto the bed.

"Suck your boyfriend's cock while I give you a good hard fucking," Conrad commanded me from behind.

"Gladly, sir," I said, with just a little sarcasm.

"Loch." Marcus' deep voice rumbled. He didn't have to say anything more.

Putting my head down, I buried it into Marcus' crotch while Coach Conrad fed his long prick into my ass. My anal ring was used to being stretched around Marcus' big piece of meat, so it easily accommodated this new smaller version.

"Oh, fuck! That's a nice tight hole, Loch." Conrad sighed. "I thought with all that fucking that you guys were doing, that you would be stretched out and loose, especially when I saw the size of that monster Marcus has between his legs."

"Loch is always just what you want," Marcus replied with a note of pride in his voice that made me smile.

I gagged myself on my boyfriend's big unit as his coach began to saw me back and forth on his long prick. Coach had a good style of fucking, but he totally would get his eyes opened if he stayed to watch Marcus screw me.

Conrad groaned heavily and then pulled his throbbing cock out of my ass. "Flip over and let me pound this sweet hole from above," he growled.

Spitting out Marcus' cock, I flipped onto my back and pulled it back into my mouth like it was an oxygen hose that I needed to breathe. Conrad slid his wet cock back inside me as I stretched my legs onto his shoulders. He was so tall that even my long legs didn't reach comfortably, so I wound up putting my heels into the creases of his armpits.

Conrad bent me in half and began to pummel me. Marcus got close to his climax and was unable to hold it off any longer. His big hose delivered a rush of hot sticky spunk deep in my mouth and down my throat. I sucked hard, eventually gagging on the amount of hot semen that filled my mouth.

"Fuck, look at that cum hound drink your load," Conrad said in awe. He busted his nut seconds later and filled me with an equally impressive load of his own.

I didn't know what the two boys I was living with had planned, but if the rest of the summer was going to be like this then it was going to be a blast!

Chapter Fifteen

The beginning of school arrived quickly and Marcus was even more involved with football than our freshman year. He was so tired by Wednesday, that I took to visiting him on our one night of the week when we saw each other. Jeremy, his roommate, was so thrilled by the fact that we kept him up most of the night and the next morning that he began crashing with our friend Vance every Wednesday night.

Marcus Battle was making a name for himself on the football field and I couldn't have been prouder of him. The coaches were using him and a junior as part of a two-tight end system that was really working for the Tarheels. I went to each game and patiently waited for him to spend his lone day off on Sunday with me each week.

Staying busy during the week with my friends, I found myself in a really good place. I loved college and had started to take a creative writing class that I was really excited about. Most weeks, I wrote short stories with themes from what was happening in the world around me. At my professor's urging, I tried to branch out into longer stories with more complicated plots.

By October, I had written a story about a vampire who had acquired the ebola disease from a victim and was constantly losing flesh and re-growing it. Laughing at my ridiculousness, I shared it with Marcus one late Sunday after we had just fucked for the fifth time and I was unable to sit.

"It's a great idea," Marcus said to me after I had read him the story.

I looked wearily at him. "But?"

"But, it just doesn't seem very personal."

"What do you mean?" This was not what I thought he was going to say.

"I mean that even though it is a good idea, it doesn't hold any weight because there is none of you in there."

I was thrilled that Marcus was just as smart as I was and that we could have an intelligent conversation like this just as easily as we fucked. "So, you think I should write something about what is going on in my life?"

He made a weird face like that should be obvious and answered, "Well, yeah."

"I could write about us . . ."

"You could."

I was shocked he agreed. "You wouldn't mind?"

"It's your life, Loch. I don't have to agree." I could see the look in his eyes and knew that he was being honest with me.

I explained my hesitation, "But it would be about you also. Your life and mine have wound together."

"I would be honored," he said with a slight bow. "Of course, I would like to read it before you publish it or anything."

"It's just for class," I said with a snort of laughter at his ridiculousness.

"We'll see," he said under his breath. "Speaking of class, I have a biology exam next week. Want to remind me about how the digestive system works again?"

"Like you need to be reminded," I said with a chuckle as I pushed him back onto the bed and knelt between his legs. "You would benefit better from trying to find out how your nuts produce so much semen and your cock is always so hard."

"I will always listen to your teachings, Loch." My boyfriend moaned as I swallowed him whole. I had gotten much better at blowjobs in the last year and Marcus always made sure that I practiced. I knew that I could bring him to his knees with my mouth as well as my ass and I did it quite frequently.

The better Marcus played on Saturday, the harder he fucked me on Sunday and I became addicted to the pattern. Marcus dominated me just like he had the defense on the field the day before. It was amazing to be a part of this sexual experience and it was like a drug that I had to have. On the days when we didn't see each other, for me it was like being in a fog for days on end. I constantly wanted to know what he was doing and plotted how I could be with him more. It was almost too much — too painful.

The pain was only relieved when I was with Marcus. My brain only shut down when he was with me. I was really starting to question myself — my sanity and my purpose — until I started to write.

At first, I just started to document how Marcus and I met. But then, I began to branch off and write stories about things that were to come and events that hadn't happened to us, but were fantasies of mine. I found my anxiety was reduced and I was more at peace with myself when I was without Marcus as long as I was writing. Somehow, it kept the connection between us open and I was grateful for it.

Marcus seemed to love my writing and constantly asked me to read sections to him. He was as supportive of my writing as I was of his playing and it really helped our relationship to have the dual pastimes.

At the end of the season Carolina was selected to play in a bowl game in Memphis over the winter break. I promised Marcus that I would be there to watch him play and he reminded me that he couldn't hang with me until after the game. I told him that I was used to being ignored and he did not think I was funny in the least, but I could tell he was glad that I was planning on coming to Memphis.

Marcus left for Memphis the week before the game on Friday and I checked into the team hotel on that Tuesday. Marcus was able to get me a room and game tickets through the University so that the whole trip wouldn't cost me so much. Although Marcus texted me that he was glad I had arrived safely, I did not see him.

I joined some Carolina fans at the hotel bar and quickly made friends with some of them. We made plans to meet up for the game on Friday.

Knowing better than to bother my footballer boyfriend with texts and calls, the next day I kept quiet and enjoyed looking around a city that I had never been to before. Memphis was awesome and I enjoyed the food, shopping, and architecture. I was afraid to go out at night by myself, so I had to skip experiencing the amazing nightlife. I watched American Sniper on pay-per-view and spent the night writing.

I was surprised by a knock on the door at eleven-thirty. Looking through the peephole, I was even more shocked to see Marcus on the other side of the door.

I swung the door open. "What are you—"

Marcus slapped his rough hand across my mouth and he propelled himself through me into my room. I recognized his mood immediately and closed my mouth against what I wanted to say.

My boyfriend must have sensed my recognition of his feelings, because he let go of my mouth. He pulled off my shorts and t-shirt without a word. Holding his arms over his head, he let me do the same thing to him.

Almost tenderly, Marcus put his big hand back onto the side of my face and rubbed his thumb across my lips. I knew what he wanted, but I also knew what he needed. He needed a connection with me and there was no better way to do that than to assume our favorite position.

Pushing his big chest with both hands, I toppled him onto

the bed and then dug in my toiletry kit for a bottle of lube. Marcus' big horse cock was already hard as a flagpole. I ran my hands over the sensitive skin of his shaft before paying special attention to the velvety-smooth cock head.

A beautiful, golden drop of pre-cum appeared in Marcus' piss slit. I looked up into his hazel eyes as I felt the lustful need rolling off of him. His eyes were imploring me to help him.

Leaning down, I let my tongue take a great wet swipe across the super-soft skin of his cock head. I left a trail of saliva behind but picked up that golden drop of man-goo and savored it in my mouth like a fine wine.

A groan of disappointment rose up from Marcus' chest. The last thing I wanted to do was to disappoint him, so I quickly lubed my hand and started to stroke his hot spark-plug. His groans soon turned to moans as I was beginning to relieve the pressure built up inside of him. I'm sure my big football player boyfriend would love for me to just complete the handjob I was giving him, but I was in this for myself as well and also needed a release.

Letting go of Marcus' hot cock, I climbed onto the bed, straddled his ripped body, and lowered myself down onto my knees on either side of his crotch. Reaching back, I maneuvered his slickened joint against my rosebud and pushed back onto it.

It was like being electrocuted, except with the shock coming from the inside of my body. Marcus and I had such a strong physical connection that anytime our skins touched it was electric, but when his giant dick invaded my ass, fitting me like a key that was made for my lock, the sparks were mind-blowing.

A huge deep rattling moan escaped from Marcus' chest as my ass wrapped around his cock like a velvety-soft glove, touching every nerve ending on his shaft and head. I bounced up and down on his pole and then his muscled arm wrapped around my chest and pulled me down onto his broad one.

Marcus was already sweating, but he held me in place on top of him as he began to fuck me from below. He was so pent up that he soon put his hands on either side of my cock and balls and lifted me off of him before pushing me back to meet his body as he jackhammered up into me.

It was an amazing fuck where my dick flopped onto one of his hands and then onto the other, I marveled at how Marcus was more involved and more physical this year. Marcus didn't last long under this pressure. He blew his load deep inside me, spraying my anal chamber with hot sticky spunk.

I lay back on his broad chest and breathed in deeply, listening to Marcus doing the same. Without any warning, Marcus rolled us over and flattened me onto the mattress with his hard body. His cock was already throbbing and engorging with blood again, even as it was still buried to the hilt inside of me.

Marcus pushed down on the small of my back, lifted his torso off of me, and began to fucking destroy my ass again. He fucked me so hard that a deep throated moan rose out of me as my cheek pressed against the mattress.

The footballer, pumping my ass like he was running a two-minute drill, hesitated for just a second before he resumed. He moved a huge paw to the side of my face and pressed down.

I guess Marcus doesn't want me to make any sound . . .

I smiled into the mattress. I found his silence extremely hot, but what turned me on more than anything was Marcus' absolute control and domination of me in those moments. He directed the action and made his wishes known, all without uttering a word. It was raw and physical and I loved every second of it.

Marcus was able to last much longer this time and used every minute of it to pound my sweet asshole relentlessly. As he got closer to his climax, Marcus lay all the way down on me, wrapped a muscled arm around my throat and pulled my head back to meet his. Burying his big blue-veiner inside me as far as he could, he released another torrent of hot cum into my bowels.

My cock was as hard as if it was made out of rock, with a flesh sleeve over it. The constant sawing back and forth of Marcus on top of me had done nothing but give me a friction boner and I was ready to blow. My orgasm happened seconds after my boyfriend's piss slit opened wide to deliver his salty present to me.

I pumped a huge load of hot jizz onto the hotel mattress beneath me as Marcus' body weight delightfully crushed me. I hummed softly as pleasurable sensations tore through my body. Having his weight on me, his big cock stretching my sphincter, his length firmly planted all the way inside me, his hot cum leaking out of my ass, his hairy muscled arm against my lips as I kissed it, and my own climax delivering pleasure right to my brain was almost more than I could take. This was my drug and I wanted it all day, every day.

Marcus made small grunting noises as he undulated his hips back and forth. He was obviously enjoying how tight my ass had become with my climax. Probably without even realizing it, he was sending me into a whole new realm of pleasure with his ever-hard dick fighting against my ever-tight hole. We lay frozen in that position as we both tried to catch our breath. This was my man and I belonged to him. There was no doubt in my mind about that and I was pretty sure that he felt the same way.

Chapter Sixteen

Marcus and I had just had a very intense fuck session and now we were lying spent on the hotel room bed. There had not been one single word uttered for the last hour.

I looked over at him and rolled onto my side, propping my head against his warm chest. Lazily, I played in his copper-colored chest hair with one finger. "That kinda broke your rule." It was strange to hear my voice after so much silence.

He chuckled, saying, "Yeah, it did. Shattered it."

I laughed, enjoying riding his chest up and down as he spoke and laughed. "You needed it."

"Just me?"

"Me too, but you really needed it," I countered.

He shrugged and said, "Hey, I just came in for a quick blowjob to ease the strain."

"I know, but I could tell you needed something else."

He absent-mindedly ran his fingers through my hair. "How did you know that?"

I rolled my eyes and answered, "Please!"

His eyes narrowed and he asked, "Did you just roll your eyes at me?"

"Yes, sir," I said with a gulp at the end.

"Hmmm . . . .perhaps there is something to this idea of punishing you when you are bad," he purred.

"Punishing or rewarding?"

"Is it the same for you, Loch?"

"Sometimes," I answered with a snort. "We probably shouldn't talk about it now. Your focus needs to return to the game."

"You do know what's best for me . . ." Marcus pried himself off the bed and smacked my sore ass with his open palm, making a sharp slapping sound that left my butt cheek stinging.

"I do and you for me."

"I think so," he said as he pulled on his clothes. "I just don't know anyone who is in the same position as me."

"Doesn't Norris have a marked boyfriend?" I asked, referring to the current quarterback who was banging the only other marked guy on campus.

"Not this year. That guy got called to Service."

A ripple of excitement ran through me. "Really?"

"Yeah. Norris is kinda devastated." Marcus hung his head and then looked up at me through his eyebrows. "Will that happen to you?" he asked in a whisper.

"No! Now go get your head in the game, Battle," I chided him.

"Yes, sir," he said with a smile forming on his handsome face. He moved towards me, put a rough hand on my jawline that was marked with the bright blue line that announced to the world that I was sexually attracted to men, and ran his large thumb over my cheek. "Thanks for that, Loch."

"No problem," I responded, a little uncomfortable with this level of intimacy. "Now, get out of here before I tell the coach what you have done."

"You wouldn't dare," he growled, knowing that it was against the team rules to have this type of distraction.

I shrugged and said, "I might need to be punished . . ."

"Not today, Loch, not today," Marcus said, grinning broadly as he repeated a favorite statement of ours, headed for the door.

I spent the rest of the night soaking in the tub in very hot water, trying to soothe my aching ass. Of course, I over-thought every single word and action that happened and couldn't help smiling at the thought of each.

We lost the game, but Marcus played very well and I was super proud of him. It took the team a really long time to return to the hotel and my body was ringing with nervous energy waiting for him.

Finally there was an aggressive knock on my door. Running to it, I couldn't get it open fast enough. Once I did get the chain removed and flung open the door, there was Marcus and another big guy.

It was Ken Farmiga. He was the other tight end that Marcus had been partnered with for the season. I hadn't met him personally, but I knew who he was from the time I had spent with the team and in the locker room. Like Marcus, he had blossomed physically over the last year.

Holding my hands out, I gave Marcus a big hug. "You did so well."

"Thanks, Loch." He uncomfortably shifted to the side and introduced me, "Loch, you know Ken?"

"We haven't met officially, but I know him. Nice game today, Ken," I told him as I gave him a high-five.

"Thanks! Your boy and I tore it up today, but we still came up short." Ken had a nice smooth speaking voice that reminded me of a news reporter.

"Next year," I said, backing up to let them into the room.

Marcus shut the door behind him and said, "I was hoping Ken could join us in a little celebration for the end of the season." He had a look on his face that appeared like it was a mix of shame and lust.

I had no problem entertaining his friend because I knew Marcus was going to be there and that it would make him happy. I would be happy just being with him and of course, having his huge donkey-dick stretching my ass wide open for hours didn't hurt either. "Cool," I said, looking from Marcus to Ken.

Ken was pretty freaking handsome. A year older than Marcus, he was just slightly taller. He had blond hair that was cut short and a matching blond beard that he had just grown out this year. Overall, he had a very Irish look to him that was quite attractive. His biceps bulged around his t-shirt sleeves and I noticed that his muscular arms were shaved smooth of hair.

"It's all right?" Ken asked in disbelief.

"Sure. I thought Marcus would probably want to have Vance or Jeremy or both of them come back with him, but the great Ken Farmiga will do just nicely." I winked at Ken to let him know that I was just kidding around with him.

"Vance and Jeremy are going out to a Service Station with the guys from the O Line," Marcus informed me.

"God bless those men working in that Service Station tonight," I said with a chuckle.

"Thank you both for this." Ken turned to me and said, "Loch, you have to know that all of us grunts on the team are jealous as hell of Marcus."

I looked at Marcus and shook my head slightly with a self-righteous look on my face.

Ken continued, "To have a piece of tail that you can fuck whenever you want is a dream we all have."

I saw the frown appear on Marcus' face as he took exception to what I guessed was the vulgarity of Ken's words. "Well, sorry to burst your bubble, Ken, but Marcus can't just fuck me whenever he wants."

"He can't?" I saw Marcus shoot me a look filled with curiosity as Ken questioned me.

"No, I have to want to fuck also." I turned to Marcus and smiled. "Marcus is just lucky that every time he wants to, so do I."

Marcus laughed out loud and slapped me on the back. "Yeah, and we want to a lot!"

"And you don't mind if I join in?" Ken asked.

I looked at Marcus and he didn't object so I said, "It would be our pleasure . . . well, my pleasure to have you join us."

"Mine as well," Ken said, with a huge grin forming on his face.

"Well, let's get to it!" I said with excitement as I reached for Marcus' shirt and tugged it off in one quick movement. Stepping over to Ken, I did the same thing and revealed his huge hairless chest.

Ken's skin was so light and smooth, like a figurine of a person. He was incredibly well-built and his nipples were small pink buttons that were just begging to be sucked.

"Sit on the bed and Loch will take our shoes off," Marcus said with some command.

I smiled coyly at him, knowing that he was setting me up to be able to worship both of these stud's large feet. The boys sat down and I knelt on the thick carpet between them, putting one of Ken's size fifteen feet into my lap. Beginning with Marcus' foot, I pulled off his slide and then his black athletic sock. I massaged his gorgeous foot with my hands, making it crack and pop under my digging thumbs and powerful fingers.

Marcus couldn't help but moan as I manipulated his foot. Pulling his foot up, I buried my face into it and breathed deeply of his masculine smell. My dick got hard instantly. Not being able to control myself, I stuck out my tongue and took a great swiping lick of the bottom of his foot.

Closing my eyes, I savored the taste of my boyfriend's foot and the electric spark that ran from the skin of his foot to my tongue. I turned to Ken and saw his eyes widen in lust.

"Fuck!" he said in awe. "I didn't know it was all this, Battle."

"We're just getting started, Ken," I said as I untied his tennis shoe and pulled his sock off. Unlike Marcus, Ken had not taken care of his feet and it showed. His foot was big and masculine, but that was all it had going for it.

I massaged and licked his foot anyway, even as I sent a look at Marcus to let him know that I didn't like it. He smirked at me and I knew that he knew exactly what I was thinking.

Standing back up, I turned on the TV to a music station, finding something suitable, and then did a very slow strip tease for the two players, making sure that as I dropped my shorts, I turned my body to show off every bit of my money-maker.

Hearing Ken give a long whistle, I smiled to myself as I once again faced them and dropped to my knees between them. Hooking my fingers into Marcus' waistband, I pulled his shorts off with a little help from him lifting himself up. I repeated the procedure with Ken and was satisfied to see that he had a nice fat cock.

Marcus' teammate looked over into Marcus' crotch and said, "Fuck, Battle! You been giving him that big hog of yours for two years and you expect him to be tight for me?"

"He'll be the tightest twat that you've ever fucked, Formiga, but regardless, I don't expect him to be tight for you. I expect him to be tight for me," Marcus said with such absoluteness that it made my cock hard as a rock.

And I will be.

Leaning forward, I sucked Ken's fat prod into my hot mouth. Taking turns, I gave them both the best blow job that I could, using my hands to continue to stimulate one of them while I was blowing the other.

Ken and Marcus came within seconds of each other, pointing their hard lances at my face. They both exploded with their climaxes and hit me squarely on each cheek. Closing my eyes, I opened my mouth and let the hot spunk fly inside.

I thought it was almost more than Ken could take as I sucked his sensitive organ. Marcus jumped off the bed and ran to the bathroom, bringing back a wet washcloth that he used to wipe my face. I cleaned him up as a thank you. Afterwards, Marcus directed me onto the bed.

I put on quite a show for Marcus and Ken. I wanted to make Marcus proud of me, of course, but I also liked performing for someone new. The fact that his fat cock stretched my hole as much as my boyfriend's did was just a bonus for me. Ken talked through the whole thing and was very complimentary of me and of Marcus' ability to dominate me.

Ken left a very satisfied part of the team!

CHAPTER SEVENTEEN

Marcus and I were both flying out Sunday afternoon, so we spent the night and the next day together in Memphis. I loved exploring a new city with him. He was interested in everything that he saw and we spent hours listening to bands and trying different bar-b-que joints. Every place we stopped gave us free beers, even though we were under age, when they saw Marcus' size, asking if he had just played in the game.

We were feeling no pain by the time the sun set and somehow we ended up in a local tattoo studio. It seemed clean and the employees, while being totally covered in tats, were very professional.

"What are you going to get?" I anxiously asked Marcus. I was concerned that he was going to get something stupid that I would have to look at for the next two years. An image flashed in my head of a tattoo of someone's face or of a giant cross.

"I don't know. What are you going to get?" he countered.

"Who says I'm getting one?" I blurted out. "This body is my ticket," I said as I moved both hands in a sweeping motion over my body.

Marcus rolled his eyes at me. "We're both getting one," he said with finality.

"All right, if it matches yours."

"Matches? What do you mean?"

"You know. So that they are two parts of the same thing or similar to each other," I suggested.

I could tell by the expression on Marcus' face that this had never occurred to him before. "Like what?"

"I don't know . . . like if you got a football with UNC on it, I could get a Tarheel with UNC on it."

He wrinkled his nose at me and then the tattoo artist suddenly appeared from behind a curtain.

He was tatted and pierced to the max. "You guys ready? I'm Jaziri." He quickly looked from Marcus to me. I saw his eyes as they met mine and then immediately went to the mark on the side of my face. He quickly darted a look at Marcus and I could see that he was impressed.

"We're ready," I said.

"Come this way," he said as he disappeared behind the curtain, motioning for us to follow.

Once into his studio, we took a seat and the tattoo artist took a hard look at both of us. "So, what you guys thinking about?"

Marcus looked at me and then answered, "We were just talking about and thinking about doing something together."

"Shit, man! Let me guess. Like a fucking key and he's going to get a lock?"

I laughed out loud and said, "Hell, no!"

The tatted and pierced guy turned and looked at me with a startled expression. "You gonna let your Servant just speak out like that?"

"He's not my Servant," Marcus said firmly.

"And no, we're not going to get bicycles built for two or connecting puzzle pieces either," I said, rolling my eyes.

"Wait. He's not your Servant?" the artist asked Marcus while pointing a finger tattooed with an ink pen at me.

"No. We're just friends," Marcus said immediately.

"But you're fucking, right? I've inked a bunch of Masters and their Servants and you two have that look and vibe."

"We're fucking . . . a lot," I said as I laughed.

"I thought so," Jaziri said with relief. "I'm pretty good at reading people and I thought I was losing my touch there for a minute."

I looked at the tat artist and asked, "Jaziri, you said that you've inked other . . . couples before?"

He nodded his head in agreement.

"What do they usually get?" I asked.

He contemplated my question for a few seconds and then said, "All the ones you named, a lot of keys and locks, some more graphic."

"Really?" Marcus asked, suddenly interested.

"Yeah. Mast and Serves are really obsessed with their cocks and assholes."

I snorted. "Who isn't?"

"True," Jaziri answered. "So, what can I do for you guys?"

Marcus and I looked at each other blankly.

"Do you want a tattoo of my asshole?" I asked with fake seriousness.

Marcus shrugged and said, "Well, it is my favorite thing about you."

I immediately rammed his shoulder with mine as I frowned at him.

"Kidding," he said before laughing.

"What do you guys have in common?" Jaziri asked, trying to help us to decide.

"Fucking," we both answered at the same time.

The tattoo artist rolled his eyes and asked, "What else?"

"We go to school together," Marcus answered.

I added, "We both like sports and school."

"What school?" Jaziri asked.

"Carolina," Marcus answered quickly.

"That's it!" I said suddenly as an idea hit me.

We were soon the proud owners of two new tattoos, both replicas of famous University of North Carolina landmarks.

Marcus had a very phallic looking copy of the Kenan Bell Tower on his side and I had a beautiful rendition of the Old Well on my left pectoral above my heart.

"It's appropriate, I think," Marcus said to me as he looked closely at Jaziri's handiwork on my chest. His bell tower was covered with gauze and Vaseline.

"You've been trying to find the bottom of that well for two years now," I smirked back at him.

"How 'bout I get a little dip into that well?" Jaziri asked as he fondled himself under his leather apron.

"No thanks, Jaziri," Marcus was quick to answer. "Our buzz is wearing off and we need to crash. We've got early flights tomorrow."

"Oh well, it was a pleasure anyway," the tat artist said with class. We shook his hand and Marcus paid him.

It was a short walk back to the hotel and to my room. Once inside, I turned to Marcus and said, "Thanks for not making me have sex with Jaziri. He was kinda creepy, but nice."

"I would never make you do something like that," Marcus said with an expression of hurt on his face.

"I know, but if you asked me to, I would."

"I already feel a little ashamed for bringing Formiga with me last night."

I smiled at him and said, "Don't be. It was fun. I just didn't want to deal with Jaziri's nappy dread locks touching me and God only knows what his dick looks like."

Marcus looked relieved. "You know that you can tell me no."

"Easier said than done. I always want to please you. If I know that you want something or it would make you happy, I am almost bound to do it for you," I admitted.

Marcus stepped closer to me and put his big hand on the side of my face again. "I want you to do it for yourself."

I looked down and said, "I do it for us."

He reached between us and groped his crotch. "I've got something else for you to do for us."

"Always," I said with fake exasperation.

He chuckled as he pushed my shoulders down and I fell to my knees in front of him. I grabbed the heel of his Timberland boot that he kept unlaced and pulled it forward. It easily popped off and then I pulled his short sock off. I did the same thing to the other foot.

"I don't want to give you a big head or anything, but you are so much hotter than Ken Formiga," I said looking up into his golden eyes.

"He's bigger and more ripped than me."

"But you take so much better care of yourself, and his cock couldn't even compare to yours."

"Like his feet?"

"Yeah," I said with a chuckle.

He scrunched up his face and said, "I could tell that you didn't like them."

"I'm used to yours, which are absolute perfection, by the way."

"Thanks to you."

"What do you mean?" I asked, searching his face for an answer. I knew that I had not done anything to his feet.

He smiled down at me. "When you have a marked guy that is worshipping your body the way you do mine, I have a certain obligation to keep my shit in order."

I laughed. "And oh how your shit is in perfect order!"

He growled, "Now, it's time for you to inspect the bell tower."

"Yes, sir. I always wanted to take a ride up the bell tower," I said with what I hoped was as much innocence as I could muster.

Marcus made a sound of pleasure and said, "I'm going to drop a load of bell-juice into your stomach and then another one deep inside the Old Well for luck. And then I'm going to keep that sweet hole of yours stretched to the limit for the entire night. What do you think about that?"

My voice was low and soft when I was able to catch my breath. "I think that sounds like heaven." Pulling his sweat pants down, I pushed my face into his boxer briefs that barely contained his bulging monster. I inhaled deeply and savored the scent of my man.

CHAPTER EIGHTEEN

Marcus kept his word to me in that hotel room in Memphis. He filled me full of semen and then I fell asleep spooned against him with his giant unit stretching my asshole open all night long.

My ass was on fire the next day as I tried to cram my big frame into a narrow airplane seat to fly home to Charleston. I already missed Marcus and couldn't wait until winter break was over when we would be reunited.

The rest of my time-off at home went quickly as I visited friends and family and generally just relaxed. I had resumed writing about Marcus and I, since I had a lot more experiences lately to document. Being able to write about Marcus helped me not miss him as much and I frequently read passages to him at night over the phone. He often made suggestions or asked questions that made me revise and rewrite, which I found to be quite helpful.

Once back in Chapel Hill, Marcus and I settled into our semi-annual new routine. Now that football season was over, we had a more relaxed routine where we spent more time with each other. That helped both of us to remain on an even emotional keel. I made sure not to ignore either my friends or his as we frequently included them in our plans.

I had started my second creative writing class and found it to be even more challenging, which I loved. Marcus was heavily into his major, accounting, which I found to be extremely boring, but kept that to myself. He hardly ever asked for help, but the higher level math was kicking his butt. He knew it came naturally to me, so I wasn't surprised to find him at my door several times late at night needing help. The math always turned into sex, since we both could concentrate better after fucking.

Marcus and I began to make plans for Spring Break with his roommate, Jeremy, and their teammate Vance. Vance's family owned a vacation home in Florida that we had used last year. The week had been great except for a beach party we had attended where a jealous bartender had drugged us in an attempt to snatch me away from my friends.

It had been scary, but we had survived with only hangovers thanks to my father's constant training on how to protect myself from NOMARs. I seemed to always be on the alert for trouble. Jeremy and Vance joined Marcus and I in my dorm room one Sunday afternoon to make some plans.

"Smells like sex in here," Vance said as I opened the door for him. I had been afraid of that since Marcus and I had been fucking all morning. I had opened the windows to try to air it out, but to no avail.

"Get used to it," Jeremy told him. "Marcus and my room smells the same way."

"Don't be hatin'," I said. "I got pizza on the way, so I'll prop the door open."

"So, what do we want to do this year?" Vance asked. "I mean, we can go back to my family's place if you guys want to, but I would understand if you didn't want to."

"I wouldn't mind going back to Fort Lauderdale," I said.

"Me either," Marcus chimed in.

Jeremy shrugged and asked, "Where'd you get the pizza from?"

We all laughed at him, knowing that his thoughts rarely left his stomach.

"Doughboy's," I answered. "What's our other options?"

Vance shrugged and said, "We could fly to the Bahamas. Dad will let us use his jet."

"Just how rich are you?" I asked, with my mouth open in shock.

"Richer than even you will be when you get that big paycheck from your Master!" Vance said, laughing.

Marcus ignored the comment from Vance, knowing that he could never afford to have me as a Servant. "Does your father have a place in the Bahamas also?"

"No, but my uncle does and he won't mind if we use it," Vance said nonchalantly.

"Fuck! We're there!" Jeremy exploded, just as the pizza guy appeared in the doorway. "And it's here!" he added quickly.

Marcus jumped up with his wallet and paid the delivery guy.

He might not have been able to afford the million dollar a year price tag that I would fetch from The Service, but he did try to take care of things when I was with him, which I appreciated. Occasionally, I would slip twenties into his wallet when he was in the shower or asleep to make up for the deficit.

The boys and I sat around eating pizza, drinking beer, and talking about the things we could do in the Bahamas. Vance had visited the islands a bunch, of course, so he would steer us clear of things that were a waste of time and make sure we hit all the hottest spots.

"The Service Station in my Uncle's plan is really hot," Vance said, right before taking a big bite of pizza.

Jeremy dropped the slice he was holding. "What?" When he saw that Vance was still chewing and couldn't answer, he continued, "Your unc's place has its own Service Station?"

A Service Station was a place run by The Service, the same organization that maybe one day might make a contract of service between me and a Master — for millions of dollars. I had delayed entering into The Service to go to college, but I always knew that the opportunity was there if I needed it. Service Stations were places where NOMARs can go to have sex, since they cannot afford a Servant.

Usually Service Stations contained party rooms that you could rent out. These basically consisted of a weird-shaped wall with rubberized circles in different positions called glory holes. A man would stick his cock through one of the rubberized circles and either receive a handjob, blowjob, footjob, or a tight ass to fuck.

It was tradition in our world to take your son on his thirteenth birthday to a Service Station to lose his virginity. The mark appeared on the exact moment of your birth, thirteen years later, and many fathers were ecstatic when their sons' faces remained unblemished. My father was worried when my bright blue mark appeared, but he took me to our local Service Station anyway for my first fuck. He had the good form to be proud of me that day and I have been grateful to him every day since.

Service Stations provided jobs for thousands of guys and many of them were not even marked. Down and out NOMARs could make a lot of money by letting someone fuck them, so they often worked in the stations willingly. Others were sentenced to work there for committing some crime. As with any business, each station was unique and customized for their clientele.

Vance swallowed and said, "His house is in a gated community and the lot of them share a Service Station."

"Wow," Marcus said in awe.

I shot my boyfriend a look like *what-are-you-wowing-for, you're-not-going-to-need-it.*

"It's impressive," he said to me while nodding his head.

I narrowed my eyes at Marcus and turned to get support

from Jeremy and Vance. I noticed immediately that Vance's eyes twinkled with mischievous knowledge.

"What?" I asked with more than a little irritation.

"They have this special rule there. When you are twenty, you can arrange to take a Bahamian boy home with you for the night."

I was stunned. "What the fuck? I've never heard of that."

"It's true," Vance defended himself.

"Marked guys?" I asked, suddenly very interested.

"Yes. Since Bahamian boys can't join The Service, they have worked out this special arrangement for them."

I hadn't realized that they couldn't join The Service. "It's how they make their money then. It must be really expensive to take them home," I said to myself as I worked out the logic of it out loud.

"It is, but I will treat, if we want to do it," Vance said with a shit-eating grin on his face. "Since we are all of age now."

Jeremy's eyes were completely glazed over with lust and Marcus was careful to hide his emotions behind his standard serious face, since I was staring daggers at him. Even though I would be jealous as hell, I would gladly let Marcus fuck someone else if he wanted. I was confident enough in my abilities that I thought Marcus would always come back to me.

"Holy fuck! Yes," Jeremy said, almost drooling.

"Should be fun," I said dryly.

"Would be," Marcus agreed.

I tore my gaze off of Marcus and said to Vance, "I'm surprised that you weren't planning on going there all along since you just turned twenty this year, Vance."

"We don't all have a hot piece of ass to hit every day like my studly friend Marcus over here. I've had it planned all year," he admitted before smiling broadly and tearing off a slice of pizza.

We all laughed and high-fived him. It was decided. At the

end of March, we were going to Nassau. Several of us had to get passports, but Vance took care of everything else.

CHAPTER NINETEEN

Spring Break came quicker than any of us could have imagined. I had started to take introductory courses in my major, psychology, and I was enjoying them just as much as I was my second creative writing class. However, I was ready for a break from school, as well as some uninterrupted free time with Marcus.

I honestly didn't know how Marcus and I could possibly fuck more than we already do, but I was very anxious to find out if it was possible. The four of us boarded Vance's private jet at the Wake County Airport within an hour of my last class. We had all been packed and ready so that I walked right out of class and directly into the waiting car at the curb that contained my friends and our luggage.

The private jet was a great way to fly! The trip was quick and easy and the plane's seats were so much more comfortable than any I had ever sat in before. Vance had a van from his uncle's community waiting for us at the airport and we were soon carrying our luggage up the walk of a beautiful beach bungalow.

The whole back wall of the house opened onto the private beach. The wall was completely open when we arrived and the view was stunning — all rocks, palm trees, white sand, and beautiful blue water.

"Wow!" I said in disbelief.

"You'll have a house like this one someday, Loch," Vance said with a sly smile.

This was the second comment from him about me entering

The Service and being rich one day. It made me excited to think about the possibility of it, but at the same time, it was presumptuous and I wanted him to stop.

He continued after a pregnant pause, saying, "Battle, you and Loch can take the master bedroom through here."

Marcus immediately put up a protest. "You should have the master because it is your place, Vance. Loch and I can take a smaller room."

"I appreciate that, Battle, but that's the biggest bed and you two definitely will need it."

I tilted my head to the side at Marcus, as if to say, *you know he's right.* "Thanks, Vance," I said to break the stalemate. "But if you want it, tell us now."

"Nope, I'm good. Jeremy and I will be back here on this side of the house," Vance said as he picked up his bag and walked to the other side of the living room.

"Get your suits on!" Jeremy shouted over his shoulder as he followed Vance. "We're going out to the water."

We were soon in the ocean, playing around with each other, blowing off steam from the flight and the second semester of school. The fridge had been fully stocked with beer when we arrived, so we started to catch a buzz in a hurry.

"Is that wall to your house always open like that?" Jeremy asked, looking at the bungalow from the water.

"No, of course not," Vance said, laughing. "The housekeeper was here this morning and I asked him to leave it open for us."

"What's down there?" Marcus asked, pointing to the beach to our far right.

"That's called Market Square. There's a really nice fishing pier, beach restaurant, bar, and open-air market."

"I could eat," Jeremy said, rubbing his big belly.

"When can't you?" Marcus asked.

Jeremy looked hurt for a second and then Marcus grabbed him around the neck and tried to dunk the big mountain of a man. Jeremy easily shrugged him off like a pesky fly.

"We can go eat," Vance said, starting to walk out of the water and up to our chaise loungers.

"How safe are we here, Vance?" I asked, once we were drying off.

"How safe?" he asked, looking a little confused.

I rephrased, "How safe am I here?"

A shadow of concern crossed Marcus' face and he asked, "Is there any danger, Vance?"

"There's always crime, but not in this community. The Bahamas are a safe haven for marked men, former Servants flush with cash, so the laws here are very strict and nothing inappropriate is tolerated."

Marcus turned to me and asked, "Why do you ask, Loch?"

"I was going to stay here and lay out . . . get some sun."

"I'll stay with you," Marcus immediately said.

"No, you go have fun with them and let me lay out. If Vance says I'm okay, I will be."

"You sure?" Marcus asked, his hazel eyes boring into mine.

"I'm sure. I'll be right here when you guys return," I assured him as I stretched my towel out on my chair and lay down.

"Keep your cell phone in your hand," Marcus advised me.

"Will do," I assured him, showing him that I had it there within easy reach. "Will you bring me back a sandwich or something?"

"Yes," they assured me.

The boys grabbed their shirts and headed down the beach. I lay down on my stomach and drifted off in the hot sun. I woke up when I heard voices on the beach and just assumed that it was my crowd coming back.

Flipping over onto my back, I sat up on the lounger and got

my bearings. It wasn't my boys, but it was an older couple who were talking as they walked down the shore line. They walked past me with just a nod of their heads.

I had already spotted the blue marks on their faces, but they didn't seem to have registered mine yet. They were in white linen shirts and hats. I had never seen marked men as old as these two, so I was probably staring a little after they walked past me.

Hearing them say something to each other, they soon stopped and turned around. They approached me without hesitation.

"Well, dahling, what do we have here?" the first one asked.

I was unsure of whether he was talking to me or his partner. "Hi," I said, swinging my legs onto the sand and sitting up.

"You're new," he said.

"And young," his friend added enthusiastically.

"I'm Loch. Just arrived today."

"Michael," he indicated himself with a hand. "This is Louis. And you are staying with Art?" he asked while looking at the house we were staying at.

The one he called Louis looked shocked and asked, "Art has a new Servant and didn't tell us?"

I assumed that Art was probably Vance's uncle. "I'm here with his nephew."

"Vance is here?" Louis asked, giving his partner a knowing smile. "We live right down the beach three houses away."

I immediately started to process what that look might mean. "Yes. We're down for Spring Break."

"And Vance is your Master?"

"No. He's just a friend of mine from school."

"From school? The SA doesn't allow NOMARs like Vance," Louis said with confusion.

I was ready for this statement. It was one that I had heard

from other marked men in the past. "I don't go to a Service Academy." I smiled at the astonished looks on their faces, as if I had just slapped them.

"Dahling, say it isn't true," Michael said, sitting down on the lounge chair beside mine. "At least you have entered service and are awaiting your opportunity."

Now, I was just enjoying playing with them. "I have not."

Both of them clutched their chests, with gobsmacked expressions on their faces. "You are giving it away to young Master Vance for free, dahling?" Michael finally was able to ask through his disbelief.

"Sometimes," I said coyly.

Just then I saw their eyes dart over my shoulder and I turned to see my three friends walking towards us from down the beach. Marcus carried a bag and my stomach growled in response at the sight of it.

"Michael, Louis!" Vance yelled as we got closer. He hugged them both and introduced them to Jeremy and Marcus as friends of his uncle.

Marcus handed me the bag and said, "Here's your sandwich, Loch. I have to go to the bathroom bad. I'll be back."

Jeremy said, "I'm right behind you."

"Bring me a beer when you come back please!" I yelled after them. Turning to Michael, I said, "I don't know if I want to eat it, if it's going to make me rush to the bathroom like those two." I noticed that Vance and Louis had moved down to the water and were deep in conversation.

Michael's eyes were on Marcus and Jeremy as they walked to the house. "Let me guess, dahling. Tall, muscled, and handsome is yours."

I grinned from ear to ear. "He sure is."

"He looks like he could hurt a boy," Michael said, fanning himself.

"He certainly could," I agreed, laughing.

Michael turned his attention to me and said, "Well, you certainly are a breath of fresh air for us, Loch."

"Thanks! Glad to be here."

Michael's eyes twinkled with delight. "There's a gala this weekend that I would like you boys to come to."

"That's very nice of you, but I don't know if we are fit for a gala . . ."

"Nonsense. It is for a charity of mine and you will love it. I'll have an invitation sent over and will pay for your table. I won't hear anything else about it," he said with finality as he stood up and swept over to Vance and Louis.

They talked for a minute and then continued down the beach, waving their goodbye to me. Vance joined me, sitting on the lounge chair beside me as I dug into the bag and unwrapped a BLT and pulled out a bag of chips.

"Louis used to be my Dad's Servant a long time ago."

"He was the first guy you ever fucked?" I asked blatantly.

Vance stared at me in disbelief. "How do you know that?"

"We marked guys can tell those kind of things," I said with a sly smile.

"Really?"

"No, not really!" I replied, laughing. "I just deduced."

He looked at me with new respect. "You're smarter than you look," he said, joining in with my laughing. "What did Michael want?"

"He has a charity event that he wants us to go to, a gala of some sort. He said he would send us an invitation and pay for us to have a table."

"Christ! Wonder what it will be this time?" Vance looked up at me and said, "He's big into charities for marked men and comes up with these crazy ass theme parties to raise money for them."

"I don't know what the theme is, but I think it is a super cool charity and I would probably want to help with it." I finished my sandwich, looking out on the beautiful ocean view and then said, "I'm going to go take a nap with my man, Vance. You staying out here?"

"Yeah, man. Have fun."

Once back in the house, I grabbed a bottle of beer from the fridge and quietly slipped inside the French doors of the master bedroom. Marcus was lying on the king-sized bed in full naked glory. His cock was hard and sticking straight up like the mast of a ship.

"I didn't think you would ever get here." Marcus' voice was so deep and his growl came from deep inside his chest, causing my heart to rise into my throat. I immediately felt the familiar burn in my balls that was always the signal for the start of a hard-on.

"You in pain, baby?" I asked seductively.

He adjusted his hard-on straighter and said, "Yes, sir."

"Let me see what I can do to help you," I said, crawling onto the bed and lying down beside him with my face at his crotch. Feeling the heat pour off of him before I even touched his skin, I licked my lips in anticipation. The sun had already kissed his skin and made it a burnished copper that had me absolutely salivating.

Wrapping my fingers around the base of Marcus' flagpole, I ran my wide tongue from root to tip as he moaned behind my back. I sucked on just the big cock head, exploring all of its treasures and sipping the sweet pre-cum that it produced.

The sparks flew immediately from his skin to mine, causing my lips to vibrate on his satiny cock head. The electrical stimulation ran right down into my balls, causing me to start leaking clear pre-cum as well.

With a loud groan, Marcus put his hand on the back of my head and forced my mouth down onto his cock. My lips stretched as the shaft of his monster plowed into my mouth and hit the back of my throat.

A humming noise rose out of me as I tried to deep throat the huge beast that had invaded me. I accomplished the feat more than once as I pumped my head up and down on him. I felt his cock twitch and expand on my tongue and I knew he was close to an explosion.

Marcus held my head down as he arched his back and he exploded into his climax. He pumped quarts of hot salty semen into my mouth and directly down my gullet. I swallowed as fast as I could, but there was no way I could keep up with the torrent of man cream that he produced.

Finally, his climax dwindled to a dribble. Pulling his still-hard cock from my mouth, I licked the excess splooge from his shaft and milked more of it out of him by digging my thumb into the big vein running along the bottom of his glorious joint.

"There. That should make you feel better," I finally said as he tousled my hair.

"Almost perfect," he said, still with his lust-filled voice.

I knew from that voice that my work here wasn't finished. "Is there something else I can do for you, sir?"

"You can sit up here where I can see you better."

"Said the wolf to Little Red Riding Hood."

He sported a huge grin and said, "I won't let anything bad happen to you."

"Only good things?" I asked as I grabbed a tube of lube from my toiletry kit and greased up his big rod.

"Really good things," he promised as I straddled his bottom half, reached behind me, and placed his gloriously big cock head onto my puckered hole. I loved riding him where I could see him.

Marcus held my hips as I pushed down and impaled myself on him. "Fuuuuccccckkkkkk!" I groaned as I slid further and further down onto his enormous fence post.

"So fucking tight!"

Holding my balls up and out of the way with one hand, I began to pump my body up and down on my boyfriend's long thick unit. Marcus surprised me by running his hands over my chest while I fucked myself on him. He even pinched my nipples a few times and smiled when my body jerked in response. My cock hardened even more.

I was enjoying the added sensation of him touching me, when Marcus pulled me down into his chest, hugged me tightly to him, and then proceeded to fuck me so hard from below that I thought I would get a friction burn from it.

His smell was amazing and we were soon sweating profusely, despite the tropical breeze blowing through the open windows. I sucked the sweat off of his hairy arm. I loved having my lips on his skin at the same time that his oversized cock was stretching my anal ring almost to its limit.

Usually, I liked to squeeze Marcus' dick with my ass muscles each time he pulled out of me, but he was fucking me so fast that it was impossible to react each time, so I just lay there and enjoyed the performance.

The rhythmic thrusts soon had my hard cock rubbing back and forth across Marcus' firm belly. My climax built until I was unable to hold it anymore. Pumping a big load of hot cum right onto Marcus' belly, I whimpered through my release. Immediately, I felt my asshole tighten like a vise around Marcus, who grunted his satisfaction.

By the time he was ready to come again, my ass was on fire. "Put it in me deep, Battle."

Marcus was unable to talk, but he followed my order and buried his entire length inside of me before he released the pressure and shot strands of hot spunk all over my anal chamber.

Marcus' arms relaxed and my body unfolded on top of him. I slid to his side and kept my head on his heaving chest. "You won't ever get tired of this, will you Battle?"

"Tired of your sweet tail? There is no way in hell," he said with a snort and smacked my ass with a big paw. "Won't you get tired of me first?"

"Why? Cause we marked men are all cock whores?" I asked teasingly.

"No," he immediately answered. "I just don't want you to miss out on anything."

I sat up so that I could look into my man's face. "The only thing I would be missing out on if I was riding someone else's cock is this," I said as I fisted his fat joint.

"As long as you're sure, but I'm still going to bring the occasional guy home to keep you regular."

"If you must," I said with a laugh.

CHAPTER TWENTY

The invitation to Michael's gala was on our kitchen table the next morning. Since Marcus and I were busy using his morning wood to pound my prostate until we both lost our shit and blew huge loads of hot cum, Vance and Jeremy got to it first.

They were all smiles when we finally emerged from the master bedroom to the smell of coffee and bacon. "What?" I asked, slightly irritated that we weren't in on the joke.

Jeremy said, "Your invitation came . . ."

"The invitation wasn't the only thing to come," Vance added snarkily, taking a jealous glance at Marcus and me.

"*My* invitation?" I asked, confused by his use of the pronoun.

"Yeah, yours," Vance said as he handed it to me.

Marcus and I sat down on the barstools and looked at the invitation. It was elegantly engraved on heavyweight card-stock made from very fine linen.

Michael Numfeld requests the honor of your presence at a charity gala.
Benefitting the Marked Man Society of Nassau.
A Charity Auction of NOMARs
Marked men may bid on the man of their choice.
$1000 a plate or $1000 to be bid upon.
Sunday the first of April at the Civic Center of Nassau.
Dinner served at 7:30

"What does that mean?" Marcus asked, looking at Vance.

Vance shrugged and answered, "I think a bunch of NOMAR studs pay to get up on stage and if a marked man in the audience wants to buy time with them, they put in a bid."

"A monetary bid?" I asked.

Marcus raised an eyebrow and asked, "You interested, Loch?"

I flushed under his gaze. "Just wondering."

"Uh-huh," Marcus said, grabbing a piece of bacon off of the island and taking a big bite of it.

Vance let me off the hook by finally answering, "I think the marked guys bid with their time."

"Their time?" Jeremy asked, confused.

"Yeah. I think they bid how long they are willing to fuck around with them."

"And the longest bid wins?" I asked. It didn't make any sense to me because I assumed that if a marked guy wanted one of the NOMARs he would be willing to spend a lot of time getting fucked by him, so all the bids would be huge.

"Not necessarily. If I remember right from the last one of those that I attended, the NOMARs are afraid of getting one of the old farts," Vance informed us. "They still get to fuck, but then they are stuck with them for days and days."

"Ah." It was fascinating to think about the strategy of the auction.

"Would you let him bid on someone, Battle?" Jeremy asked my boyfriend.

"Yeah, Marcus, would you *let* me?" I asked with extreme exaggeration of the one word.

"Loch can make his own decisions, but I think it sounds like fun. I want us to go and I want to see if there is anyone he would want to bid on," Marcus said, deftly avoiding any drama.

"Woo-hoo!" Vance said. "Looks like we are going to the big marked party."

Jeremy looked at the invitation. "It's tomorrow night."

"We'll need tuxes," Vance said. "I'll take care of it."

"Thanks for the support, guys. I will reward you all later," I said with a raised eyebrow aimed at Marcus.

"I like the sound of that," Jeremy said, with a big shit-eating grin spreading across his face.

"Why are you so excited, Vance?" Marcus asked suspiciously.

"It's a roomful of marked men and I look like *this*," he said as he flexed his muscles.

The four of us broke into laughter and sat down to eat, still talking about the invitation.

I eventually asked, "Well, if we are going to do that tomorrow night, when are we going to go to the Bahamian Service Station?"

"Maybe on Monday, so we can recover from the festivities after the gala," Vance suggested.

Jeremy looked at me and asked, "Loch, you gonna let Battle have a marked guy for the night?"

"Of course," I answered immediately.

"You're not worried?"

"Battle has been a good boy. He deserves a little . . . variety." The boys all laughed. "Besides, he ain't gonna find someone there with a sweet hole as tight as mine."

"He's probably right about that, Battle," Vance joked with the big guy.

"It's a tall order, but I will commit myself to sticking my big cock in as many asses as it takes to prove Loch is right," Marcus said, with a wink in my direction.

I snorted with laughter. Loving that Marcus was just as clever and smart as I was, I slapped him on the back of the head and then tried to strangle him with my arm around his throat.

"It's the least we can do," Jeremy agreed.

"Let's go to the beach," I said. "I need a tan!"

We spent the rest of the day in and out of the ocean, only going back to the house to eat and get more booze. The four of us got along really well with each other. I showed them how much I cared for them late in the afternoon, when I lowered myself down on my knees onto the heavy dark wood of the outdoor shower.

"Bonus," Marcus said as he stripped his board shorts off and pushed my forehead back until my face was pointed up and our gazes connected.

I loved when Marcus took control and dominated me. He did just that as the water fell all around me and he used the other hand to pull my jaw down. That simple move opened my mouth. Marcus smiled down at me and then moved his thumb from my chin to my lower lip.

His caress of my lip with his large thumb was so intimate and so unlike him that it made me horny and uncomfortable at the same time. My cock filled with blood and rose between my legs.

My boyfriend suddenly slipped his thumb into my mouth and hooked the corner. Marcus lifted his thick cock and dipped it between my lips like a candle-maker dipping his wares into a pot of hot wax. I wanted to close my lips around my prize but his over-sized thumb kept my mouth open.

When he spoke, his voice was husky and ragged. "You want me to control you, don't you, Loch?" He pulled his cock back out of my mouth.

"Yes, Marcus," I said, in a voice laced with lusty need.

"Yes, *sir*," he immediately corrected.

My eyes narrowed at his, but I saw a light radiating from his eyes that stopped me short. He was absolutely delighted to dominate me. He wasn't kidding or trying to do something that he didn't really feel. It truly was what both of us wanted.

"Say it," he commanded. My cock responded by getting so

painfully hard that I thought it would explode as it clung to my belly.

"Yes, sir." My voice sounded so strange to me with those two words. I recognized it as a combination of need and relief. Almost like I had been waiting for this moment for years and now that it was finally here, I was extremely satisfied. I had said the two simple words before, but this was the first time that I had meant it.

"Good boy," Marcus said with his sex voice as he lowered his dick back into my mouth and removed his thumb. His cock was a strange color. Darker than normal, it was obviously engorged with blood but there was something different about it.

This was my reward for being good. Sucking his cock was a treat for me and he had used it as a reward for allowing him to establish his dominance, and I was perfectly okay with that.

I gave him one of the best blowjobs he had ever had even as I jacked my own cock. We both came within seconds of each other, releasing huge loads of sperm. Mine went down between the large spaces in the slotted floor boards of the outdoor shower and Marcus' went right into my stomach. Marcus' load was the largest one he had ever produced with me. It was even bigger than the very first one he gave me at the start of our freshman year when he finally relented and fucked me for the first time.

I was just starting to lick his big fishing pole clean when Jeremy and Vance entered the shower. They had stayed behind at the beach to give us time to take our showers without all of us being crammed in there together.

"Well, fuck, what do we have here?" Vance asked with a smirk.

"Looks like your uncle's outdoor shower has a new feature," Jeremy said dryly.

I didn't let their appearance rattle me, not while I had hold of Marcus' cock and I was busy cleaning it up with my lips and tongue. They weren't going to make me miss that opportunity.

"Can we have a go, Loch?" Vance asked with a cocky tone.

I took the last suck off of Marcus' cock head and looked up at him.

Marcus hesitated for a second and then said, "Loch will take care of you boys."

"Hot damn!" Jeremy crowed. Vance responded only by removing his bathing suit faster than lightning.

Marcus leaned down, placed his thumb back into my mouth, and whispered into my ear, "You give them a good blow, Loch, but you do not let them come in your mouth. You understand?"

I nodded my head.

He continued, "You are mine and I am the only one who is going to keep you full of cum at both ends. Do you understand me?"

"Yes, sir," I whispered so quietly that I wasn't sure Marcus had heard it. He was surpassing everything I had ever hoped he would be and I was absolutely thrilled with him.

My football god straightened back up and removed his thumb from my mouth. I watched as he grabbed a towel and started to dry off on the side of the shower. Vance and Jeremy had taken his place, but Marcus' gaze never left me.

I had plenty of time to process what had just happened between Marcus and me as I serviced his two teammates who were also my two friends. Taking turns working one of them over with my mouth while I rubbed and stroked the other one with my hand, I soon had them hard as steel beams and leaking deliciously clear pre-cum that I couldn't get enough of.

Marcus had surprised me with his command and when he said that I belonged to him, it was almost more than I could take. Those words made shivers run up my spine and excited me more than anything anyone had ever said to me before.

Jeremy's fat cock was the first to twitch and explode with his climax. He tried to hold my head steady with both hands as I took long drawing pulls on him, but I thwarted him. Pulling his cock out of my mouth, I stroked him with both hands as I kept his cock head buried in my cheek. He came in a torrent of hot spunk that I let the shower water wick away from my face.

"Fuck! Battle is one lucky son-of-bitch," Jeremy said, finally able to speak again.

"I don't know. I think I might be the lucky one," I said in opposition.

"Well, I want to be the lucky one," Vance whined.

Vance's long cock was next. Just like Marcus' big hog, there was no way I could completely deep throat the whole thing, it was just too long. I resorted to teasing his head—running my tongue into his piss hole, around the foreskin between shaft and head, and sucking hard just with the head inside my hot mouth.

Vance was at my mercy almost immediately. He wanted to hold me down and face fuck me so I let him by moving over to the wooden fence that surrounded the shower. Putting my back against it, I let the rich kid furiously fuck my mouth until he was on the verge of his climax.

"Oh, my fucking God." Vance moaned with his eyes closed, his head up and back, and his hands on the sides of my face. He had his long fingers dug into my hair, fisting it as leverage.

Vance came in an explosion of power, just as I was able to remove his cock from my mouth and place it on my face. Sucking his pale balls covered in brilliant red hair into my mouth, I felt his long member start to spew hot spunk over my head and down my back. He came a lot, but soon dribbled his spunk onto my forehead. I pumped his long shaft with my hand, milking more of his cream into the water headed towards the slats in the floor.

"You are amazing, Loch," Vance groaned.

"It's the least I can do for letting us come to this beautiful place of yours, Vance."

"One day, I hope to have a Servant who is just like you." He said it so softly that my heart went out to him. I hoped that Vance got exactly what he wanted.

CHAPTER TWENTY-ONE

The next night, we showered and dressed in the rental tuxedos that Vance had delivered to our bungalow. Marcus looked positively edible in his black cotton suit with a red tie. My tux was grey with a silver vest and a silver tie.

"I'm so going to fuck your brains out later with the image of you in that tux still on my mind," I promised Marcus.

"Now that's a promise I'm going to make sure you keep," he growled.

"You look fantastic," I said, suddenly a little fearful of unleashing my handsome boyfriend into a room full of marked men.

As if he could read my mind, Marcus said, "Don't worry, Loch. Tonight is all about you. I'm just your eye-candy."

I laughed and agreed with him by shaking my head. "The most handsome eye-candy ever."

We soon joined Jeremy and Vance out in the living room. They also looked very handsome in their suits and we took a ton of selfies with our cell phones to document the occasion. Vance had called for a taxi which took us to the gala.

The Civic Center was lit up with lights in the palm trees and a red carpet up the stairs. The four of us drew a lot of stares as we made our way inside the event. The marked men salivated over the young athletes and I imagined how the older ones were gossiping about why a marked man was with three studs in their prime.

We flashed our invitation at the door and were pointed towards our table. I was ecstatic to feel that the center was air conditioned, since I was already starting to sweat through my three layers of clothes. Having never seen so many marked guys in one place before, I didn't know who to look at first. I was used to being the only marked man wherever I went, and now I was just one of many in this grand ballroom.

Having just sat down, I saw Michael and Louis as they approached our table with a bottle of champagne.

"Dahlings," Michael called. "You look positively charming."

"Thank you so much for the invitation, guys," I said immediately. "It was really too much to pay for our dinners also."

"You don't have your cash yet, young one," Louis said to me. "We can afford to indulge you a little bit until that happens."

"Well, we appreciate it," Marcus said without hesitation.

I looked at Marcus and wondered if their comments about me entering into The Service had an effect on him or not. I still didn't know how I felt about it, but had been too chicken to bring it up and find out for sure. I was sure that he would feel conflicted about it just like me.

"You are welcome," Louis graciously said.

"Here is your program, Loch. We thought you might want to do a little window shopping before the show begins." Michael winked exaggeratedly at me and at Marcus. He handed me a thick program that felt like a Broadway playbill.

We chatted for a few more minutes until four new men entered, who turned out to be our table mates. Michael and Louis greeted them as well and then quickly excused themselves to work the crowd. Taking seats at our table were four marked men, two in their thirties and two in their forties. They seemed like two couples to me, but I couldn't be sure.

Our table mates were curious about why we were here and why I was not in The Service. I told them my story and they frowned at my delay of entering The Service. Those frowns turned to downright disapproval when I told them that Marcus and I had been together for two years.

Fortunately, our first course arrived and the smell of seafood bisque filled the air. I noticed that the stage was built so that it was wide across and also protruded out into the middle of the room with an extension. Our table was not directly along the stage but was one row back from it, so that we would be able to have a pretty good line of sight.

The second course was a salad that contained a conch fritter on the side. The two parties at our table had settled into two separate conversations. The rest of the food was just as delicious as the first several courses, but none of it had been too much. The dessert was a beautiful mango panna cotta that was to *die* for.

After dessert, I was able to look at the program and was delighted to gawk at all of the NOMARs that were up for auction. Each of them had a small photo and a one-page biography. If I thought I was shocked before, it was nothing compared to how I felt when I saw that each NOMAR had a row of personal statistics next to their picture.

I quickly looked for a key to the different symbols that were shown. The first one was a red square with the number forty-two in it. The key said that this was his age. The second symbol was a blue circle with a picture of a bear in it. According to the key this meant that he was hairy. A white diamond meant that he was wealthy and a yellow rectangle contained his height and weight. A bent arm was next and the key said that meant he was *skinny muscled*, whatever that meant. The last symbol was what looked like a black thermometer with the number nine beside it. Looking down at the key, I saw with shock that the number represented the length of the NOMARs cock and the thermometer represented his girth.

Reading the lines under the picture, I saw that the biography held the NOMAR's name, occupation, ancestry, and a section on his favorite sexual fetishes and proclivities. It was a very provocative read. Flipping through the pages, I marveled at the lengths of the cocks and some of the freaky things that the men were into. When I looked up at Marcus and saw that he was watching me, I felt my face flush bright red.

"What are you up to, Loch?" he asked in his deep voice that penetrated the very core of my being.

I leaned over and showed him the program, pointing out the symbols that I was looking at and also the section on their fetishes. Marcus read them with a smile on his face and then gave me a thumbs-up just as the lights dimmed and *Uptown Funk* started to blare out of the speakers.

Suddenly there was a flood of NOMARs onto the stage. They were dressed in every outfit you could imagine from costumes to formalwear. There were firemen, athletes, policemen, businessmen, skateboarders, swimmers, construction workers, and cowboys. It looked like the Village People family reunion. The marked men in the crowd went berserk—clapping and cheering.

There was no big dance number like I had expected when I saw all the NOMARs on the stage, but instead they moved to designated spots and then slowly switched to another spot on the opposite side of the stage so that everyone could get a good look at them. Soon, the curtain dropped and Michael walked out from the wing of the stage to a podium off to the side.

Michael thanked everyone for coming and for supporting his charity. He explained that if you saw a NOMAR that you would like to bid on, you should send your offer via text to the number on the front of the program. His suggestion was to make an offer that was specific to your desires and wishes to increase your chance of success. He ended by saying that he didn't want to waste any of our precious shopping time, so he started the show.

Vance, Marcus, and Jeremy were looking at me when I turned back to the table. "What?" I asked.

"Nothing," Marcus said. "It's just good to see you in the opposite of your normal environment."

"Now we kinda know how you feel all of the time," Jeremy said.

Vance had been fending off marked men's attention all night and the other two had certainly had their fair share of admiring fans as well. Most of the marked men were respectful of me when they learned that Marcus and I were a couple, but I was enjoying seeing them flirt with my man, and his reactions.

The music started and Michael announced that this was NOMAR one, which drew a laugh from the crowd. The program said he was *Joe from Miami*. Joe was dressed in a suit and really worked the runway when he had the chance. He must have been a catch, because I saw a lot of the marked men at the tables furiously texting on their phones. I guessed that a nine-inch dick was a prize too good to pass up.

"Are you going to bid on him?" Marcus asked me, leaning in.

"No. I don't like his hair," I said with a smirk. I reached over and pushed his hair to the side off of his forehead.

Marcus smiled and gripped the back of my neck, slowly massaging it. My whole body warmed as bolts of electrical charges flowed through me from my man's hand against my skin.

There was a round of applause as Joe left the stage. Michael announced NOMAR two and a swimmer in a Speedo came out to applause. It didn't take long before the Speedo was off and the man was completely naked on stage. He had a nice long cock that had the marked men going crazy trying to text their delight to him.

The boys at my table were impressed and discussed

whether they could ever have the nerve to do that.

"In a room full of marked men? I certainly could," Vance said.

"That's because you are a man-whore, Vance," I said with a smile.

"Said the man who is going to bid on a man to fuck him tonight when he has one already with him," he shot back.

I shot a worried look at Marcus to see if I had misread the situation. His expression was his usual non-readable one. "I only want to bid if Marcus says it is okay."

"I want you to bid," Marcus said, squeezing my neck. "You will see that no man matches up to your man and you will come back to me in gratitude."

Jeremy and Vance laughed out loud, but I just stared at Marcus because that was the same way I felt about him being with another marked man.

"You sure?" I asked, just loud enough for him to hear me.

"I'm sure," he said. "In fact, I command it, so you better make that bid good." Marcus' eyes blazed at me in the semi-dark of the ballroom.

"Yes, sir," I said, swallowing hard and shifting uncomfortably as my cock hardened in my tuxedo pants.

With the introduction of the third NOMAR, I noticed that a large screen at the top of the stage started to flash up the winning bids starting with NOMAR one. It saddened me to learn that the first winning bid contained a thousand dollars offered to the NOMAR. There was no way I could offer money.

The next NOMARs onto the stage were two firemen and they were a package deal. They had removed their shirts and just had their fire coats and suspenders on over their muscled chests. The crowd went wild and the second winning bid flashed up. Not only did this one offer some money, but also an extended amount of time—the marked man was going to allow the NOMAR a whole weekend of sex. There was no way I could compete with that, either.

Resigned to just have fun with my bid and not worry about it, I cheered and shouted for the NOMARs as they tried to dance or get the crowd excited about them. Some of the winning bids were quite vulgar and it made me blush with embarrassment for the writers, but the crowd seemed to love it.

We were ten or so NOMARs into the auction when Marcus leaned over to me and said, "Here's the one."

I quickly looked to the stage and saw a tall thick construction worker walk out. He carried a jackhammer over his shoulder and his plaid shirt was unbuttoned all the way to his dirty jeans, revealing an amazingly muscled and hairy chest. Marcus certainly knew my tastes.

I turned to Marcus, smiled, and shook my head. Leaning into him, I said, "He's no Marcus Battle, but he will do."

"Well, there's only one Marcus Battle," he said with a laugh.

Quickly flipping to the man's page in the program, I saw that his name was Mark from Ohio and that his cock was nine and a half inches long with medium girth. He was into hard fucking sessions in public areas that lasted for hours at a time. *Wow!*

"You know how much I like my Ohio boys," I said to Marcus.

"Really?" he asked with an appreciative nod of his head.

While Mark began to simulate jackhammering on stage, I composed my text. It basically said that while I couldn't offer any money to him, I would offer up to five hours of incredible sex like he has never experienced before. I signed it with my bidder number from the front cover of my program and hit *send*.

"Did you get it done?" Marcus asked as Mark left the stage.

"I did. Now, we wait and see!" I said excitedly.

The construction guy's bid came up several minutes later

and he had gone for the offer of a car. I was bummed but Marcus' conciliatory hand on my back made it all better in a hurry.

A half hour later, a short guy in a suit came onto the stage to a smattering of polite applause. He was in his late thirties, but looked older than that. Even though he was short, he was real beefy with a thick neck and a powerful body under that suit. The crowd didn't seem to be paying him much attention and I saw this as an advantage for myself.

He wasn't bad looking at all and had a swagger that I really found attractive. He had a bald head and wore a grey suit with a black shirt that was unbuttoned down to the middle of a muscular chest. He walked to the middle of the stage and flexed for the crowd. I could see veins that were well defined on his hands as he made fists. He had friendly eyes with well-defined brows, a hint of dark facial hair, and big ears that made him look a little like a cartoon character of a beefy meathead.

I checked the program and saw that he was a UFC MMA fighter named Dana White. He had an eight-inch cock that was super thick and was into anything that goes.

Looking up at my table, I saw that Marcus was occupied with an older marked man who was simply fawning over him. I grabbed my phone and sent a quick text.

I can't offer you money or a car, but as the youngest marked Guy here tonight, I can guarantee you that I have the tightest Ass in this room. I will give you five hours of uninterrupted Sexual pleasure.

I re-read the message before sending it and decided to add something to appeal to his MMA nature.

Willing to be bound in submission or ready to bind and Dominate you at your say.

Hitting the *send* button, I finally exhaled. No one had seemed to notice and when my bid came up as the winning bid ten minutes later, no one said a word to me.

The show came to a close. Marcus leaned over and said, "Sorry, you didn't get a NOMAR tonight, Loch."

"I got one," I replied back with a grin.

"What?" he asked, shocked. "Let me see your phone."

I handed him my phone and he read the text. I slid over the program opened to Dana's page.

"You like him?" Marcus asked in surprise.

"No, I like you, but he might be fun to fuck with."

"He's not who I would pick for you," Marcus said in deep thought.

"He probably thinks I will submit to him, but it will be me who will be in charge."

"You like to be in charge?"

"Not with you, but with others who don't know what they are doing, yes."

"Well, good luck," he said awkwardly.

I was about to respond that I didn't have to go through with it when someone yelled from the crowd.

"What about the stud at table nine?" the yelling man repeated as he stood up. I recognized him as the guy who had been flirting with Marcus.

"We're table number nine," Jeremy said in shock.

Chapter Twenty-two

The crowd in the ballroom at the Nassau Civic Center suddenly got very quiet. Someone shouted, "Yeah, if he can keep that young mark happy, then he certainly can keep me happy for a night!"

Someone else added, "Let us bid on him, Michael!"

I knew that these men were talking about Marcus from the second that they yelled. Michael looked our way from the podium. I could tell by Marcus' face that he had no idea that they were talking about him and I loved him for that. Vance, of course, thought they were talking about him.

"Who?" Michael called into the microphone.

"The big one!" someone yelled, and the crowd laughed in unison.

"You," I said to Marcus.

He put his finger to his chest and asked, "Me?"

"Yes, you big lug. They are asking for you," I told him as I flashed him a big smile.

"Marcus Battle?" Michael asked.

Marcus turned to Michael and said, "I don't have a thousand dollars for the buy-in, I'm afraid."

"I'll pay his way!" someone shouted.

"I'll split it with you," another one joined in.

"All right, settle down and keep your tongues in your mouths," Michael said to calm the rowdy, partially-drunk crowd. "We don't even know if young Marcus is willing to entertain one of us for the night." He paused for dramatic effect and then asked, "Marcus, could you join me up here,

148

please?"

Marcus was startled as the whole ballroom was staring at him. I saw the steeliness rise up in his features as he came to the conclusion that he was going to have to go on stage. What I didn't see coming was what he did next.

Standing up, Marcus straightened out his tux and then grabbed my hand. He pulled me into a standing position and then tugged me after him as he took off towards the stairs to the stage.

"What are you doing?" I asked him quietly, totally embarrassed.

"You're going up with me," he said with his flat affect used for occasions just like this.

"Why?" I whispered back.

Marcus didn't answer. We had to walk all the way across the big stage to join Michael on the far side. I could hear the marked men in the crowd as they buzzed with chatter and judged us.

"An added treat," Michael said into the microphone. "Marcus has brought up his boyfriend, Loch. Do you have to ask his permission, sweetie?"

Marcus leaned over to the microphone. "I don't have to ask his permission, but Loch is very important to me and he will be the one reading the bids and choosing the winner. So, be careful," Marcus warned the crowd, who immediately broke into loud applause and excitement.

I felt like shit for not letting him select the NOMAR that I bid on tonight, now that he had so magnanimously let me do so for him.

The crowd retrieved their phones and someone shouted, "Tell us about him, Loch!"

Michael handed the microphone over to me and I stuttered at first, not knowing what to say. "He . . . Marcus . . . well he is a sophomore at the University of North Carolina where he is an excellent business student and a member of the varsity football team."

A cheer went up from the crowd.

"He is originally from Ohio. He is six-feet-four-inches and three hundred pounds."

"What's he like in the sack!" someone yelled and the crowd fell into a fit of laughter and talking.

"He's the most amazing fuck I have ever had," I said, looking into Marcus' deep golden eyes. "And I've had a lot!" I added for comic relief. It worked and soon the crowd was on my side.

"Marcus and I have been together for almost two years and he is one of the kindest men I have ever met. He's funny, compassionate, grounded, smart, hot, humble, and loyal to a fault."

Another shout from the audience, "Sounds like you are in love with him."

I hesitated and then said, "I think I am, so you bitches can step off. I'm going to take him home for myself!"

"Now, Loch," Marcus quickly said, grabbing the microphone. "This is for charity." Marcus had followed the line of my joke and was adding to it. "Besides one of these NOMARs tonight is going to be keeping you busy, so I'm going to need a little something-something."

The crowd roared with delight and I couldn't help but laugh openly at Marcus. "All right. If you have to!"

"Settled!" Michael crowed into the microphone. "Send your bids for Marcus Battle right now. And thank you for helping out our charity tonight, boys."

We nodded our heads and Marcus ushered me back to our table where Vance and Jeremy were waiting to high-five us. Even the marked men who were sharing our table with us had lightened up and told us how well we had handled that.

Champagne was being passed around and soon someone

brought Marcus a printout of his bids. I read them over his shoulder.

You can fuck me for one year starting tomorrow.

I will give you a thousand dollars and let you fuck me for a week.

Unlimited vacations in one of my homes in the Bahamas, Vegas, Connecticut, and LA for sex with you for the rest of your vacation here.

I will arrange for an internship with any brokerage firm on Wall Street and a job when you get out of school for seventy-two hours of uninterrupted sex with you.

My Master was a powerful executive with one of the NFL teams. I can make sure that you are invited to training camp if you spend a week with me now and another one with me over the summer for the next two years.

I will blow your big cock like a fucking vacuum cleaner. Better than that tight-assed young guy you are with ever dreamed of doing.

I'll let you fist my hole all night long.

There were a couple of others, but they were mostly repeats of what had been promised before. I felt like Marcus had a tough choice on his hands based on the bids.

"Which one do you think I should pick, Loch?"

"It's hard. The NFL one probably would help you with your career goals the most."

"Yeah, but I'm going to do that on my own. I don't want it handed to me and besides, who wants to give up a week during my summer for two years?"

I loved that he considered getting to fuck someone that wasn't me for a week an inconvenience. "How about the thousand dollars? You could use that."

"Yeah, but we aren't going to be here for a week." Marcus looked at me, his eyes full of honesty and said, "Besides, I think taking money for fucking wouldn't sit well with me."

"Wall Street?" I asked.

"Not interested. What would you pick?"

"Vacation houses," I said a little too quickly. "That way we could all benefit from it."

"Yeah, but I would have to fuck him every day we are here."

"You like to fuck multiple times a day . . . need I remind you?" I asked with a smirk.

"You wouldn't mind that?"

"You know I want you all the time, but if you need to go fuck for an hour each day to get us free vacations, I would wait for you." I couldn't get through the whole sentence without laughing.

"I'm going to give you something to wait for," he threatened. "But I think you might have picked the best one, because it doesn't say how long I have to stay once I've busted my nut."

"That's my smart man. You sure?"

"Yeah. I can suck it up for the next four days."

"It's so hard to have two marked men at your disposal twenty-four hours a day," I said with fake boredom.

"Your mouth is going to get you into trouble, mister," Marcus threatened. His voice was so deep and gravelly that it resonated right down to my crotch as my cock began to fill with blood.

I made the motion of locking my lips and throwing away the key while simultaneously pointing at the directions on the sheet to circle the winning bid. Marcus followed my finger, picked up the pen, and made his choice. He passed it over to Vance and Jeremy who read the choices with delight.

Marcus handed his paper into the official and we watched the winning bid for him appear on the big screen. Michael came back to the microphone and announced that the auction was over and for all the winning bidders to report next door.

Next door turned out to be a smaller ballroom where a table was set up with a crystal punch bowl. Marcus and I each took a cup, finding it to contain some type of alcoholic punch. The bidders were immediately matched up with their purchases.

I saw Dana moving towards me from across the room. As he approached, I said, "Hi."

"Hey," he said, looking down slightly.

"I'm Loch."

"Dana. Thanks for your bid." His voice was very raspy.

"Yeah. No problem."

"I thought I would wind up with one of these old dudes and instead I got the cream of the crop."

I blushed and said, "Thanks."

"So, you wanna come over to my place tonight?" he asked, obviously anxious to get started.

"You will come to our place where I can make sure that you are respectful," Marcus said with authority. "I'm Marcus."

"Yeah, I know," Dana said, shaking hands with my man. Marcus towered over the MMA fighter. "I heard the things you guys said about each other and I don't want to get between that."

"And you won't," I quickly said. "You're going to get yours, but you will not have an effect on how we feel about each other."

"So, don't worry about that, man. Just have fun," Marcus said, lighting up and slapping the older man on the back.

"Here's the address, Dana. We have to meet Marcus' match and then pick up our friends, so I'll see you in about an hour. Okay?"

"Can't wait," he answered me gruffly before smiling and shuffling off.

The marked guy who had won the bid on my boyfriend approached a few seconds later. He appeared to be in his early thirties with light blond hair shaved into a faux hawk. He was of medium height, which was shorter than both of us, and had a wrestler's build under his tailored suit.

"Hi, I'm Keith," he said, shaking our hands.

"You the one that won me?" Marcus asked in a moment of self-pride.

He laughed hard and answered, "I am! It's nice to meet you guys."

I immediately pictured him naked and sweaty underneath Marcus as the cock I had come to love so much pounded repeatedly into his tight ass. It made my blood boil, but I kept my composure the best I could. I was happy for Marcus that he had not gotten some old troll.

"How in the world do you have so many houses, Keith?" I realized that it was a rude question, but I was dying to know.

"My Master was a real-estate tycoon and he gave me my money early on in my Service. He showed me how to use it to buy properties and increase it."

"That's cool!" I said with excitement, causing Marcus to shoot me a worried look that disturbed me.

"Well, yes, it is. It's left me a little cash-strapped, but I have fabulous places to go and visit. And soon, so will you."

"So, speaking of getting down to business . . . what is the arrangement you are looking for?" Marcus cut right to the heart of the matter.

"I just want to see what it feels like to be fucked again on a regular basis," Keith said nostalgically. "Of course, I used to get that all the time when I was in Service, but not so much these days."

"I would think you could have anyone you want." This side of The Service was something that I had never thought of or considered before.

"You would think, but so far it hasn't worked out that way for me." He seemed really sad, but then I watched as he exhaled and changed his attitude on the spot. "Who knows, maybe my big strapping football player is out there

154

somewhere and I haven't met him yet."

"I hope so," I said with genuine affection. "But this one is mine, so enjoy him, but he has to be returned."

"Well said," Keith said, laughing. "Tomorrow morning? You wanna work out with me and then we can see what happens?"

"Sounds awesome," Marcus said.

"You just said his magic words," I informed Keith as I slapped Marcus on his hard abs.

"Here's my card. Come to my house, say eight?"

"Keith, I'm afraid at that time that I'll still be marking Loch as mine after his wild night with his purchased NOMAR." Marcus couldn't help but smirk at me.

Keith looked at me but continued to talk to Marcus, "Are you forcing him to do this?"

"No, but he knows I want him to do it."

"Why is that?"

Marcus now looked at me also. "We feel like it keeps us . . . fresh."

"Who doesn't like fresh?" Keith asked, holding up his glass as Marcus and I clinked ours to his. "Let's say ten o'clock then."

CHAPTER TWENTY-THREE

Dana appeared at our place about an hour and a half later. Vance was already in his room fucking the shit out of some thirty-year-old rich marked man who had caught his eye at the gala. Jeremy was on the couch waiting to see what Dana looked like. Marcus' roommate had arranged to be wined and dined tomorrow by two marked men in exchange for a night of wild sex. He was in seventh heaven.

I opened the door and let Dana inside. He was still wearing his formal wear. Marcus and I had changed into shorts and tees.

"Hi," he said awkwardly.

"Hey, Dana. This is our friend Jeremy, and you know Marcus."

"Hey, man," he said to Marcus, shaking his hand again. "Nice to meet you, Jeremy," he said, grabbing his hand and pumping it.

"Dana certainly has a lot of energy," I noted to Marcus.

"Could work out well for you," he smirked.

I eyed the big man whom I was enamored with and said, "You know that you don't have to stand guard, don't you?"

"I'm going to anyway."

"Well, thanks," I said to him, unable to look away from his eyes that were blazing at me. "Do you think you and I can fuck afterwards?" I shyly asked.

"Five hours not enough for you, Loch?"

My entire face and neck flushed with embarrassment. "Yes, but I want you to mark me as yours again afterwards,"

I said, using a familiar theme from our freshman year to-gether.

"I would like that, too. Maybe we can shower together to wash him off of you after."

I grinned like a fool. "Thanks, stud. Time to go, Dana."

Dana was ready and quickly followed me into the master bedroom. "Goodnight fellas," I said to Jeremy and Marcus be-fore closing the French doors.

"It's kinda strange doing this in front of them," Dana said, once we were inside the bedroom.

"It is."

"I mean, I understand why. He doesn't trust me and I'm sure there are a lot of dangerous men out there . . ."

I interrupted him by agreeing. "A lot." Opening the sliding wall towards the ocean, I said, "We can start on the patio, if you want to." The ocean breeze felt wonderful and the moon was high enough to be able to see clearly in the dark.

"That would be nice," he said as he moved out onto the patio with me.

"Let's get you out of this monkey suit," I said, approaching him. I began to unbutton his expensive shirt and heard his breath catch in his throat. I could feel his heart pounding away inside his chest. "You've done this before, right Dana?"

"Yeah, but it always amazes me."

"I'm glad to be of service," I said, pushing his jacket off of his muscular shoulders.

"You like to kiss?" he suddenly asked.

His question caught me by surprise. I had never kissed an-yone before. Kissing was a very intimate act usually only done between marked men who were in love with each other. I considered it even more intimate than fucking or sucking someone's dick.

"I guess so," I finally said.

"I'm just asking because I like to and I wanted you to know

that in case you wanted to."

"Unusual for a NOMAR, isn't it?"

"It is, but the very first Servant I was ever with taught me and I quite liked it," he said as his face heated up with color.

"We can try it, then," I said, licking my lips and pulling his shirt off. The cuff links stopped me from getting it all the way off of him, but I did reveal his chest, which was cut and thick at the same time. His whole upper chest was tattooed and he had huge biceps for such a small guy.

Putting my palm flat on his chest, I ran it up and pinched first one nipple and then another. He didn't flinch, but instead smiled at me as I played with his body.

"Keep playing," he said quietly.

I grabbed his biceps and squeezed them hard. He didn't flinch. I held his hand and removed his cuff link, freeing the shirt from his wrist. I repeated the process until he stood before me naked from the waist up. Pulling off my clothes, I watched him looking at my ass and finally saw him flinch.

Wrapping my fingers around his muscled forearm, I pulled him off of the porch and onto the sand. I immediately dropped to my knees in front of him and unzipped his tuxedo pants. Reaching inside, I felt his hot member and pulled it out of his fly.

Dana was hard already and his average-sized cock was covered in large bulging veins. He was already leaking pre-cum from the slit in a beautiful cock head.

"Sorry for the size," he apologized.

I looked up at him as I grabbed the base of his cock and said, "Don't ever apologize for something so beautiful, Dana."

"I-I just thought your boyfriend in there probably has a really big cock and . . ."

"He has a gigantic cock," I said firmly. "But that doesn't mean that yours is not of any value," I told him. "I can't wait to ride this bitch and have you pound my ass into submission."

"Really?" he asked in shock.

"Really," I confirmed for him. "Your body is smoking and your beautiful cock will feel really good inside me. Now, shut up so I can suck on this beautiful joint."

"I thought you were willing to submit to me?" Dana smirked.

"Is that what you want?"

"Yes," he said with more than a little embarrassment.

I immediately bowed my head and rose up into The Service Squat. Even though I had never been to The Service Academy, I definitely knew the standard position for a Servant in front of his Master. It was not comfortable — head bowed, full thigh squat on my toes, and forearms on my spread thighs, but I did it.

"Fuck! That's so hot."

I could sense that he wanted me to suck his cock now, but he wanted me to submit, so a good Servant would wait to be directed. Waiting patiently, I concentrated on my burning thighs until I received direction. I could hear him taking off his pants and shoes.

"Suck me," he finally ordered, his voice so deep and gravelly that it sounded unworldly.

I moved forward and collapsed onto my knees, grateful for the change. Grabbing his cock by the base, I slowly started to tease it with my tongue — exploring everything about it. The bulging veins on the shaft gave it the look and mouth-feel of a French tickler. I salivated all over his hot rod.

"Mmmmm." Dana moaned as he stroked my hair and guided my head. "You do that really well."

I didn't respond, except to bear down on his cock and pump it even harder. His cock expanded and became harder, signaling his approaching climax. I didn't know whether he wanted me to continue or let him fuck me with this hard cock, but he wanted to control the action, so I kept going.

Dana came by pulling his dick out of my mouth and pumping his hot cum over my head. The last few strands hit me on the face while I kneeled with my eyes closed and my mouth open.

"Aw, fuck!" he spat while his body spasmed with his release.

Opening my eyes, I sat back onto my heels and waited for my next instruction. Instead, I was shocked by his next move.

Dana ran his hand over his bald head and said, "Damn! That was good." He leaned down and planted his lips on mine so softly that my first instinct was to pull away from him. I forced myself to freeze and was amazed at how nice the kiss was. Then I realized that I had his cum on my lips.

I pulled back from him and said, "Sorry, but I kinda have your cum on my lips."

"So? Don't you know that all NOMARs have tasted their own cum at some point?"

"Really? Why?"

"Curiosity, I guess."

"Did you like it?" I asked with a smirk.

"Not really. I don't know how you guys can swallow a whole bucket of that stuff," he said with a smile. "Did you like it?"

"Your cum?"

I could see him rolling his eyes by the moonlight. "No, the kiss, Loch."

"It was good," I said quickly, blushing to my core.

"Is it okay if I can do it again?"

I didn't know what to make of this short, stocky NOMAR with his average cock and penchant for kissing marked men. I was unsure how I felt about kissing him, but I did admit to myself that I liked it and wanted to do it more. I worried what

Marcus would think of it and somehow it felt like I was cheating on him, but that wasn't enough for me to tell Dana to stop. I said, "Sure."

"Good," he said quietly. There was a moment of awkward silence and then he commanded me to stand.

I stood and he slowly walked around me. He seemed fascinated with my ass, as all NOMARs inevitably were. He lightly grazed my ass cheeks with his rough hands, causing me to get a cold chill. He must have seen the shiver that ran through my body, because he smacked me on the ass and said, "Go get on the bed, Loch."

Standing up and brushing sand off of my lower legs, I followed his command.

"On your knees," he said as he followed behind me.

I climbed onto the bed and kneeled facing away from him. There was no doubt that he was ready to fuck again and I was hyperaware that I was close enough to Marcus to feel the electrical pull of his body through the screened French doors. It was a very weird feeling.

Dana climbed onto the bed and pushed my shoulders forward. Instinctively, I went down onto all fours, but he kept pushing until my face was on the mattress. Now my ass was fully exposed. Dana climbed into the saddle between my legs and spit a big loogie onto his cock and rubbed it in with one hand. With his other hand he spread my cheeks and roughly ran over my rosebud.

"So small," he whispered. "I thought that big goon out there had a massive rocket that he was firing off into you constantly?"

"He does," I confirmed.

"Yet your sweet hole is so tight," Dana exclaimed as he inserted a rough finger inside me.

"I have a special gift of tightness, you could say."

"Fucking fantastic!" Dana spit on the top of my ass and

guided the spit into my hole with another finger, spreading my anal ring further apart. "You ready?" he finally asked when he was done playing.

"So ready," I said breathlessly. I knew that he wasn't going to feel anything like Marcus inside me and he probably was not going to be able to scratch that pesky itch so deep inside my ass, but I was ready to be fucked even if it was foreplay for my time with Marcus.

Dana pushed his dick into me and my ass hole spread to allow it. My anal ring immediately clamped down onto his shaft as he slid inside of me.

"Oh fuck! That's it," Dana said with lust thickly coloring his voice.

He reached the end of his cock so quickly that I wasn't ready for it, but then he began to fuck, and it became clear what his strengths were. Dana fucked hard and fast and his hands never stopped roaming over my body while he did it — first my hips and thighs, then my lower legs and feet, my back, my shoulders, sides, chest, stomach, nipples, neck, and then my hair.

Dana fisted his hand in my hair and he soon had a handful which he used to pull me up into a kneeling position again. He kept up a constant plowing of my ass as he pulled my torso back onto his. Turning my head to the side, his lips were on mine before I even realized what was happening.

This time his lips were firm and insistent, crushing my lips. He soon had them parted and his tongue entered my mouth. It was amazing and quite over stimulating as he continued to push into me with his cock. I met his tongue with my own and explored his lips and mouth just like he was doing to me.

When he reached his climax, Dana buried his cock as far into my ass as he could and his tongue as far into my mouth. His kisses turned into a full-throated moan as he released his seed into me. His whole body jerked with his release and he whimpered into my mouth as he coated my anal channel with hot spunk.

"Shit!" Dana eventually was able to come back to himself, pulled back from me, and softly asked, "How was that?"

"Really great, Dana," I assured him.

"Your tight little ass is heaven on Earth," he told me as he began to thrust back and forth again. "No wonder your brute out there won't let you out of his sight."

"It's not that. He wants to protect me," I said, defending Marcus' honor.

"I know. I'm just kidding with you. I would do the same thing if you were mine."

"Well, I am yours for three more hours," I reminded him.

"Can we go again?"

"I am at your command," I said, saying the words that I knew would light his fire.

"On your back," he ordered as he pulled away and out of me.

I followed his command and flipped onto my back, raising my legs, bending them back onto my stomach, and locking them in place with my arms. If I thought that his last fuck was hot, it was nothing compared to this one.

Dana put my long legs onto his muscled shoulders and then entered my dark cave again with his sea serpent. He thrust his hips forward and back a few times until he had a good rhythm and then he leaned forward and covered me with his body. He held my head in place and his lips found mine again.

Kissing me like he needed it to breathe, Dana continued to undulate his body which drove his cock back and forth through my hole like a piston in a car engine. His kisses this time were long and luxurious—more one big, long slobber than kiss.

It made me a little uncomfortable, but with his constant

drilling of my ass at the same time, it was a new experience that felt exciting. He finished himself off by arching his back over me, holding himself up with his big arms, and exploding inside my ass again.

Unexpectedly, I leaned up and planted a sweet kiss on his lips as he ejaculated inside of me. I was very happy that I had chosen Dana and I couldn't wait to try to incorporate the lessons he had taught me into my time with Marcus. I couldn't even fathom what kissing Marcus would be like. I think I would explode if we kissed while fucking.

Fortunately for me, Dana wasn't finished teaching me his lessons. He pulled out of me, went to the closet, and returned with two robe belts. I propped myself up on my elbows so I could see what he was doing.

"Enough nice guy. Now, I'm really going to fuck you like you need me to, Loch," the MMA fighter growled.

CHAPTER TWENTY-FOUR

Dana kept me strapped down to the bed in various positions for the next two hours. He took his time and satisfied himself with my treasures repeatedly. He worked my ass
at one end and then came to my head and worked my mouth.
He seemed to think that he was some kind of bondage master,
but he was nothing compared to my old boss, Mr. Lewellyn,
who was a true dungeon master.

The last thing that Dana did before his time was up was to
give me my release. He untied one of my hands and let me
jack my cock until I reached my climax, dropping my load
onto my stomach.

"Fuck," Dana sighed as he watched me spew. "I wish I
could take you home with me."

"I enjoyed our time together, Dana. You were fabulous." I
told him, ignoring his wish.

"So were you."

"Can you do me a favor before you go?" I asked.

"Absolutely. What you need?"

"Can you retie my arm and gag me before you leave?"

He grinned at me and asked, "You want your man to come
and save you after you've been kidnapped and abused?"

"Something like that," I said as I returned his foolish grin.

"I can do that for you," he said as he re-secured my arm to
the bed post, and then, leaning down, gave me the softest kiss
before stuffing a sock into my mouth.

"Thanks again, Loch. I hope we can stay in touch," he said
as he entered his digits into my cell phone. Helplessly, I

watched as he went to the bathroom, showered, and dressed in his formal wear again.

I moaned the word *welcome* around the gag and watched him leave the room. I heard Marcus' deep voice in the other room and then heard the shutting of the front door. My heart was racing about what was going to happen next. Suddenly, there in the doorway of the darkened room was my man.

"Smells like shit in here," Marcus said as he stood at the door and did not enter.

"Mmmmmm," I moaned behind the gag.

"You're no victim, Loch." Marcus' voice was deeper and huskier than normal and I knew exactly what that meant. His words, however, were not what I was expecting. *Was he angry with me? Did he think that I had overstepped somehow?*

Marcus slowly walked over to the bed, his dark golden eyes missing no detail of the scene. He pulled on the robe ties and drape cords that were binding me spread-eagled on the bed. "Rise," he commanded. I was afraid to spit the sock out of my mouth without his permission, so I didn't.

I slowly stood beside the bed. I had been confined for several hours, so I was a little unsteady, but I made do. Marcus took a second to pull the ties off of my ankles and wrists. He spun me around facing away from him as my pulse pounded in my temples. Pulling my arms behind my back, Marcus tied my hands to the small of my back.

What the fuck was he doing? I was very confused and starting to get really concerned that he was mad at me.

Spinning me back around to face him, I felt a tear slide out of the corner of my eye and onto my cheek. Marcus loomed in front of me. He reached out and wiped the tear away. "Why so sad, Loch. This is what you wanted, isn't it? You've been a bad boy and you need to be punished."

I had thought that he would have rewarded me after saving me, but I guess Marcus was letting me know that once again, he was the one in charge and not me.

"You're a filthy mess, Loch. We need to get you cleaned up." Grabbing me around my bicep, he pulled me towards the open wall of the bedroom. I followed after him and soon realized that he was headed to the outdoor shower. Marcus turned on the shower and pushed me under it. There was a shower wand, which he deployed to clean me from the tip of my head to my toes.

"You've obviously forgotten who you belong to, Loch."

I knew in my heart that I had never forgotten that fact and that made me relax a bit, thinking that Marcus was playing out a little fantasy here. Marcus unscrewed the head of the shower wand and shoved the pipe up my ass with one quick movement.

The water was cold, really cold, and I screamed behind the gag at its sudden intrusion in my ass full of hot man-seed.

"Yeah, Loch. Take it. Take all of that water. You know who is in charge now, don't you?"

"Yes, Sir," I tried to say around the sock. Instead I nodded my head.

"That's right," he said as he worked the hose in and out of me. "Don't worry, Loch. I'm going to give you what you need." Marcus finished cleaning me out, turned off the water, and pulled his clothes from his body.

I expected him to dry me as I shivered in the cold wind, but Marcus had other things in mind. He approached me, bent down, and picked me up into his arms like my six-foot-three frame was nothing. He headed out between the palm trees bordering the ocean.

"The sand will scrub you clean," he told me as he lay me down on my back on the ground. Lifting my legs and untying my arms, he knelt in front of me. I felt the heat and sparks from his giant apple-headed cock before it even touched me. With one strong push, Marcus entered me. His eyes never left mine as his unlubed tree trunk sprouted inside of me.

The sand exfoliated the pores of my back as Marcus ground down onto me, smashing me with his weight. His cock continued to fill me up, making me think that it was never going to come to an end, but it did. Marcus was buried up to his short hairs inside me and I was completely filled with him.

His golden eyes swirled as I stared into them and I saw something besides lust and need. I couldn't tell what it was, but I knew we were okay. This is where I was supposed to be and with the man that I was meant to be with. There was no doubt in my mind.

"You okay now?" he asked softly.

I didn't try to talk, but just nodded my head to the affirmative.

"I told you that I would give you what you needed, Loch. You know that you can count on me for that, don't you?"

Again I confirmed it for him silently.

"Now, what was it you wanted me to do after Dana left? Oh yeah, you wanted me to mark you as mine. You still want that, Loch?"

I started to nod my head, but he reached up between us and pulled the sock out of my mouth.

"Say it," he ordered.

His cock was so thick inside of me—holding me open so wide. It pulsed and throbbed inside me, writhing like a snake caught in a bag. "I need you to mark me as yours, Marcus."

"How much do you need it?"

"More than you know."

"I know a lot about what you need."

"Please, Marcus," I begged.

"There it is," he sighed with pleasure. "I need it just as much as you do, Loch." Marcus burrowed his arms under my back and then he picked me up and crushed me to his chest. With one strong show of force he lifted me and rose to his feet until he was standing.

I was so tempted to kiss him like I had done with Dana just a couple of hours earlier, but I knew that Marcus was in charge here. He planted my back against the rough bark of the nearest palm tree and drilled his cock back all the way inside me, punching my prostate and then delving into the depths of my ass.

"Who do you belong to?" Marcus asked as he put his arms under my legs and lifted me further off of the tree.

"You, Sir," I answered breathily.

Marcus pulled his cock all of the way out of me, leaving me empty before he slammed it back into me. "Whose cock do you crave above all others?"

"Yours, Sir."

Again he withdrew and slammed back into me. "Who keeps you spread open further and longer than anyone ever has?"

"You, Marcus."

This time I braced for the thrust, but instead he smacked my ass with some force with the flat of his hand. "Who does your ass belong to?"

"You, Sir."

He slapped his hand over my mouth and asked, "Who owns this mouth and your hands?"

"You do, Sir," I mumbled against his sweaty palm.

He pulled out and sunk back inside me with force. "Whose hot cum do you need in all of your holes to feel right?"

"Yours, Marcus."

This time he leaned back and thrust his pelvis forward, basically mounting me on his cock. It caused him to be deeper in me than I had ever felt him. "Whose cock reaches up into you further than anyone's and scratches that itch for you?"

"Yours, sir."

His thrust this time almost dislodged my back from the tree, but he held me with no problem. "What do you want more than anything in the whole world?"

"To be here with you . . . like this, sir."

This time he unexpectedly thrust into me twice. "What do you need me to do?"

"Fuck me hard, sir."

Another massive thrust rocked my ass. "Whose man am I?"

"Mine. You are my man, Marcus."

Three thrusts accentuated this point. "And whose man are you?"

"Yours, sir. Always yours."

Marcus Battle didn't ask another question. Instead, he fucked me so hard and so deep that I had an out-of-body experience against that tree. He did what I wanted him to do, which was to thoroughly mark me as his and to completely erase any lingering uncomfortableness between us from my time with Dana.

What he did to my ass was so unlike anything that Dana had even tried to accomplish. It was very evident that while Marcus and I enjoyed having different experiences on occasion, we would always be drawn home to each other. Everyone and every fuck would always pale in comparison to what we experienced with each other. I knew it and Marcus Battle knew it.

"Come for me, Loch," he whispered into my ear.

"Yes, Sir," I answered, pressing my rock hard cock further into his hairy stomach. Marcus' thrusts caused his stomach to repeatedly stroke the large vein on the bottom of my shaft and it only took seconds after his order for me to fulfill it.

My climax came hard and fast, shooting cum between our big sweaty bodies like cream between two Oreo cookies. This one must have been double-stuffed, I produced so much cream.

I clamped down on Marcus' big rod with my asshole,

causing him to growl like a bear from deep within. "There it is," he hissed between his clenched teeth. "You are mine." He thrust into me twice more before exploding in a huge climax that quickly began to overflow my ass and drip out of me.

"You are mine," Marcus said with exhaustion.

I put both of my hands on the sides of his hairy face and pulled it back so that I could see his eyes. "I am yours and you are exhausted. We better get in bed because you have a morning workout session tomorrow," I reminded him.

"I just did my workout," he said with a tired chuckle.

"Yes, you did."

Marcus carried me to the shower where he rinsed us off before carrying me back into the bedroom. He dropped me onto the bed while he continued on to the bathroom. Our uncoupling left me with the most desolate empty feeling, but when he returned, Marcus spooned me and made sure that my ass was properly impaled on his stake.

We slept that way for the rest of the night.

CHAPTER TWENTY-FIVE

When Marcus' cell alarm went off early the next morning, I groaned into my pillow. Marcus, however, was up and bounced out of bed, even though he had only had an hour of sleep.

"Wanna come with me to work out, Loch?" he asked on the way to the shower.

"Fuck no!" I answered emphatically. "I don't think I will even be able to walk today, let alone work out."

"Dana too much for you last night?" he asked.

"Dana who?" I asked with a chuckle. "It was you. You were the man last night."

"That's right! I will always be the man."

"Yes, you will."

"Don't you forget it," he said, before slapping me on the ass hard.

"Ow! Fuck, Marcus!" I yelled.

"Oh, you're not kidding. Sorry," he apologized as he lightly ran his hand over my ass cheeks. "Want me to get you an ice pack before I shower?"

"Yes, please."

"Coming up." Marcus left the bedroom, completely naked, and returned with a Ziplock bag of ice wrapped in a dish-towel.

"Thanks, man."

He sat down on the side of the bed and put a big paw on my head. "You mad at me for last night?"

"Hell, no! You were amazing, maybe the best ever."

"Wow! Well, you did ask me to mark you as mine."

"Yes, I did, and you certainly completed that mission. Now get going, so I can get some sleep."

Marcus didn't move, but instead was quiet for a couple of seconds, which caused me to open my eyes and prop myself up on my elbow to be able to look into his face. "You're not the least bit jealous of what I'm getting ready to do?"

"I think I probably feel the same way that you do before you let me get fucked by someone."

"Yeah?"

"Yeah. It's not ideal, but I understand the need for it. Variety is always a good thing, but in the end, I know with one hundred percent certainty that you will return to me. You will not find what you need in that marked guy's ass or mouth, no matter how hot or tight it is. I have what you need and you have what I need. I don't know why or how, but that is the way it is and nothing you do today is going to change that."

"Well, okay. I'm glad we got that straight," he said with a jesting tone.

"Isn't that the way you feel or am I reading it wrong?"

"That's the way I feel," he said. "I just wanted to hear it from you." He winked at me, smashed my head back into the pillow with his over-sized hand, and headed to the bathroom.

I spent the rest of the day sleeping and soaking in a tub of hot water. Marcus came back to the vacation house around three o'clock and went right to the bed. He was exhausted and slept until dinnertime.

Jordan, Vance, and I had been swimming and were hanging out on the lanai when Marcus emerged from his sleep coma.

"My man," I greeted him warmly. "You must have been exhausted."

"I was."

"Vance just got up about an hour ago," I told him.

Marcus looked at Vance with respect. "You bang it out, Vance?"

"All night long," Vance crowed.

"Literally," Jordan said with a snort. "Kept me up for most of the night."

We laughed and then I asked Marcus the question that I had wanted to ask him the minute he got home. "How was it?"

"It was good," Marcus answered. He winked at me and then said, "I gave him his money's worth."

"Oh, yeah?" I asked, already feeling the jealously well up inside me like a terrible serpent.

"We worked out, grabbed some lunch, and then I fucked him three times."

"Three times!" Vance exclaimed. "I thought you got to hit that every day that we are here."

"I do, but you know, I couldn't just give him a one and done." Marcus looked at me and I wondered if he thought that I thought that he had overstepped. "I felt guilty, you know."

"You're a good man," I said to relieve his anxiety. "Are you still my man?"

"Absolutely," he said with a foolish grin. "His hole was completely loose, but oh how he could work that mouth."

"Now, you're just trying to get on my nerves," I said as I punched him on the arm.

We went to dinner at a place Vance recommended and then came home and watched some movies. The four of us excitedly talked about tomorrow night's trip to the local Service Station and about Marcus' second day of morning workouts.

Marcus took his assignment in stride, so much that I really began to question his enjoyment of it. But when he returned, he showed me how much he had missed me each time. I was absolutely flabbergasted that my man could get up early, workout like a demon, fuck Keith three or four times, then still have the energy to pay attention to me. He was so amazing that it hurt my heart to even think about it.

Jordan, Vance, Marcus and I spent the day playing golf until dusk, showered, and then went out to a late Caribbean dinner. By the time the next night rolled around, the boys were so ready to go to the local Service Station that Jordan was literally waiting in the car for the rest of us.

I was sure that Nassau had several Service Stations, but the one that Vance drove us to was unsurpassed in its grandeur. The façade of the classic building was done in deep blues and light pinks. There was a shell motif in every part of the larger than average building, reminding me of a stately mansion from the antebellum South.

We were greeted by a butler when we pulled into the covered portico and stopped the car. The butler was dressed in dark blue livery and wore white gloves. He greeted Vance by calling him *Master Vance* and asking about his father and uncle.

"Come here often or something?" Marcus whispered to Vance as we walked inside the air conditioned palace of pleasure. We were immediately greeted by someone official in a very expensive suit.

"Master Vance, I didn't know you were in town," the official said with a quick smile to all of us. He was evaluating the group in an instant like a laser light pointed at a bar code. I watched his cool, even look drop from his face as he saw the thick bright mark on my face which had been made brighter by the attention of the sun this week.

"My buddies and I came down for Spring Break, Max."

"And to celebrate your birthday, no?"

Vance laughed out loud and said, "You know it."

"Excellent," Max said, the dollar signs practically flipping over his eyes like the tumblers on a slot machine.

"Max, these are my friends," Vance said as he indicated us. "This is Jordan, Marcus, and Loch."

"Ah, and will Masters Jordan, Marcus, and Loch be in need of our special Bahamian services tonight?"

Before Vance could answer, I said, "Max, I will not be in need of anyone tonight."

Max moved towards me like he was drawn on a string. His small hand was on my mark before I even realized that it was there. "Yes, I see. And whose Servant are you, big man?"

"I'm no one's Servant, sir." Now that Max was standing beside me, I could see the very faint blue line on his dark cheek, hidden partially behind his black chinstrap beard.

"Really?" he asked in a shocked voice.

"Really, but I do belong to this one," I said with a campy wink as I smacked Marcus in the chest with my arm.

"Nice," Max said, as he took in all of Marcus Battle. He quickly turned to Vance and said, "So, we will be needing three overnight Bahamian Servants tonight, Master Vance?"

"Yes, Max. I'm going to spend my birthday money on this," Vance said with a sigh.

"No, need, Master Vance. Your father and uncle both extended you credit for your birthday," Max said with a grin.

"Score!" Vance yelled, immediately high-fiving all of us.

"Would Master Loch like to wait in our bar area while your friends are . . . shopping?" Max asked me pointedly.

Before I could even formulate an answer, Marcus answered for me, "He will be choosing my selection, Max."

Max's head whipped from Marcus to me in a millisecond. He looked at me with a new sense of respect and awe. "My, what power this one possesses."

"You have no idea," Marcus told him. "No idea."

I rolled my eyes, knowing that Marcus and I were a couple and that we shared the power and if there was an imbalance, his side was the more powerful one.

"Very well," Max said. "Follow me."

He led us to a bar area and offered us whatever we wanted to drink. Once we had a drink, Max led us to a set of grand doors and flung them open. Inside was a scene right out of *Arabian Nights.*

Chapter Twenty-six

The doors of the opulent Service Station opened onto a thrilling scene. I watched in amazement as the host walked us into a large room comprised of beds and drapes of gossamer fabric in the blue color of the Caribbean flag. The lights were low, from small lamps that must have also been covered in fabric, because the light was muted and colored.

Dark shapes shifted in the room and as my eyes adjusted, I made them out to be men. The Bahamian men were dark, but wore bright Speedos in the colors of the flag. Most of them were thin and muscular, of average height and stunningly handsome. They scrambled to get a look at the visitors, many of them falling into a fluid bodily movement that was meant to be seductive.

"These are the finest Junkanoo boys on the island," Max told us. "They are the most handsome, the most experienced, and the most skilled, of course."

Junkanoo was a term that I had come to learn was the Bahamian holiday like carnival and it also was synonymous with the word *party*. Most of the party boys were teenagers, but there were a few that were older and had kept in good shape. There was every body type imaginable and every hairstyle.

I was fascinated with this unusual set up. In the US, a Service Station only offered anonymous sex through a rubber glory hole. But here, the Bahamian boys could be hired out for the night at top dollar. Noticing that the boys were wearing different colored Speedos, it made me wonder if there was a caste system, so I asked Max about it.

"No caste system, but the colors do indicate each boy's specialty," he said to me with a small smile. He continued, "Blue is for the boy with an exceptional mouth, black is for the boy with an exceptional ass, and yellow . . . let's just say, yellow is for the boy with some special skill."

"My man has need of a boy that can handle his special skill," I told Max as I patted the significant bulge in the front of Marcus' pants.

"You want one of the yellow suits, Master Loch." Max left me to urge my friends further into the room to mingle.

I followed Marcus, but not too closely. I got propositioned several times, some more lurid than others. Guessing that it probably was common place for a lot of wealthy post-Service marked guys to hire them for the night, I enjoyed the flirtations, but rebuffed them all.

Marcus however, was hopelessly swarmed by the party boys. He was a prize and all marked guys could sense it. He greeted them all with a smile and talked with as many as he could. He avoided the ones that tried to grab his junk but flexed for the ones who wanted to feel his biceps. He was a towering figure over all of them.

Vance was having no problem getting his fair share of attention, with his handsome looks and sexy disposition. The party boys were fascinated with the red hair that he had let grow on his chin since we had left Chapel Hill and couldn't keep their hands off of it.

Jordan was having the time of his life. He sat on one of the big beds and let the guys flock to him. Twice when I looked over at him, I saw two boys sitting on his lap and his hands down both of the backs of their swimsuits while the boys giggled and blushed at the things he was whispering to them.

Marcus and I had made a sweep of the expansive room and returned to where Max waited. Marcus looked at me and asked, "Which one should I get, Loch?"

"I'm not sure. Did you see anyone who you liked or talked to anyone who was . . . stimulating?"

His golden eyes seared into my soul. "You are very stimulating to me," he growled while palming my ass in his big mitt.

"Not tonight, Battle, not tonight," I told him with a giggle.

"All right, if I can't have you . . ."

"Let's find one for you, you big lug," I said, taking his hand. I led Marcus into the seething mass of bodies and he stopped to talk to a tall skinny guy in a blue Speedo named Usu. Usu was willing to be screwed by both of us all night as long as he got to get his lips around the tremendous lap-hog that Marcus was sporting now in his pants.

Marcus raised an eyebrow at me and I shook my head. Leaning over, I whispered to him, "This is all for you, Marcus. I do not want to . . . distract you."

Marcus said goodbye to Usu and we walked towards the rear of the room. There a set of twins, barely eighteen, flirted with Marcus and hung on him from each side. They were relentlessly fondling him as they whispered all of the things that they would do to him, if given the chance.

While Marcus was busy with the twins, I noticed a guy sitting on a bed at the very back of the room. Other guys were sitting on the edges of the mattress, waiting eagerly for Marcus and me to walk their way, but not this guy. He was in the middle of the bed, propped up on the pillows, and not even looking our way. Shifting so that I could get a better angle from which to see him, I saw that he was wearing a yellow Speedo and was quite handsome.

"What's your name?" I asked, loud enough to carry to him.

"Who, him?" the Junkanoo boy in front of him asked. When he saw my head nod, he answered, "His name is Jijuri, but you don't want him."

I stepped closer. "Why not?" Jijuri's head turned towards

me for the first time.

"Because these bitches know that I am the real deal," Jijuri said defiantly.

"As if," his bedmate said, rolling his eyes.

"Can you guys give us a moment, please?" I asked, talking to the other guys on the bed.

"Who are you, Servant?" one of them snapped.

"I'm the one picking for him, asshole."

"Sorry, man. We didn't know," the asshole said.

"Sure, we'll give you some space," one of them said. "We'll just go talk to your man."

The cut was meant to hurt me, but these party boys had no idea how confident I was in my relationship with Marcus. I didn't even turn my head, I was so confident.

"Jijuri, you interested in going home with my man?"

"Doesn't matter," he answered with attitude.

"You want me to step?"

Jijuri looked at me with new found respect in his eyes. "No, you cool. You can stay."

"So, you interested?"

He nodded in the affirmative.

"Say it," I commanded.

"Yes," he answered reluctantly. "You the Master? Your man a sub?"

I burst out laughing. "Anything but!" I got my serious face back on and asked, "So why the yellow Speedo, Jijuri?"

"They call me the bottomless pit," he whispered.

"You're going to need that little talent," I whispered back to him.

Jijuri's eyes blazed with lust and he asked, "He's really that big?"

"Oh, yeah," I said, nodding and laughing.

"He is nice?" he asked in a voice that told me everything about the pain he has experienced before.

"The nicest guy I've ever met."

Jijuri looked at me like I was crazy. "You don't mind if I fuck with your man?"

"Of course I mind, but it is something that I think he should do," I told him while putting a reassuring hand on his knee.

Jijuri looked down at my hand and then back to me. "You watch or you want to fuck me, too?"

"Neither," I answered, withdrawing my hand. "This is Marcus' time. He will enjoy your talents only."

"I will do this, then."

"Good."

I stood up and Marcus soon joined me. "You have someone?" he asked.

"Yes." I watched as multiple party boys joined Jijuri on the bed.

"Thank God. I don't think I could fight off any more of these guys tonight."

"Welcome to my world, stud," I replied, snorting.

Marcus looked at me for a second and then laughed. "I never thought about it before, but this is kinda what you put up with all the time, isn't it?"

"Yes, but not as much since I got a big boyfriend to protect me," I said with a wink.

"If I remember correctly, you were pretty good at fending for yourself before me . . ."

"Maybe, but now I don't have to deal with it as much, thanks to you."

"You are welcome. Now, show me which one you like," he commanded.

"I think that the one in the middle would be interesting for you," I said, indicating Jijuri. "His name is Jijuri."

Marcus followed my eye line and asked, "Why him?"

"He has a special gift that should make it easier for you to enjoy him," I answered mysteriously.

"Is it the same gift that you possess?" He smirked.

"Not quite. But, it should be fun for you. Also, he requires a strong hand, so it will be good practice for you," I said with a snort.

"He's not the only one that needs a strong hand," Marcus growled.

"Not tonight, Battle, not tonight," I teased him. Before he could say anything else, I called for Jijuri. "Jijuri, come here."

He scrambled to obey me, quite unlike any behavior he had displayed so far tonight. He stood in front of Marcus and me. "Kneel, Servant," I snapped.

Jijuri kneeled on the thick carpet so fast that the other party boys watching gasped in response.

"This is my man. His name is Marcus and I will not tolerate anything but the best for him. Are you the best in this room, Jijuri?" My voice was firm, but not cruel — the perfect combination that I was hoping for.

Jijuri nodded his head.

"Speak, Servant," Marcus commanded, his big deep voice booming in the room.

Looking around, I saw that we had just garnered the notice of almost everyone in the room, including Vance and Jordan. They seemed to have already made their choices.

"I am the best, Master," Jijuri said evenly. "That is why the rest of these average boys resent me." The crowd in the room scoffed at him.

Marcus immediately responded by saying, "I am not your Master, boy. But after tonight, you may wish that I was."

"Yes, Sir," Jijuri answered with wide eyes.

Max had quietly slithered up to us and now stood behind the space between us. He said, "I have never seen Jijuri submit in this way before."

"Servant, my man, Loch, has given you a great honor tonight," Marcus' voice boomed. "Kiss his feet and thank him."

"Yes, Sir," Jijuri said as he bent and kissed the tops of my feet. "Thank you, Master Loch."

I stroked his bald head and said, "You are welcome. Jijuri. Do not make me regret it."

"No, Sir. I will treat Master Marcus just like I would my true Master. You will be very happy with me."

"We better be," I said staunchly.

"You have an extremely high standard to try to reach, Jijuri," Marcus told him. "Loch is probably the best fuck on this island."

"I will—"

"Do not speak unless I direct you to do so."

Jijuri nodded slightly and bowed his head.

Marcus turned around and said to Max, "This one will do for me."

I reached up and pushed Max's jaw until his mouth closed. "Don't look so surprised, Max. Marcus is a god that walks amongst us mere mortals."

"Hardly," Marcus said with a big puff of air. "Jijuri, let's go," he said without even turning around.

Jijuri and I both followed Marcus as he headed out of the room. Vance, his pick, Jordan, and his pick were already leaving. We completed the necessary paperwork and were soon on our way back to the beach house.

CHAPTER TWENTY-SEVEN

I tried to sleep on the couch while Vance, Jordan, and Marcus fucked up a storm in the separate bedrooms, but couldn't really get much more than a nominal nodding off. It wasn't that I was jealous. I didn't think I was, at first . . . but to be honest with myself, I really was. I didn't harbor resentment, but I would take Jijuri's place under Marcus in a heartbeat if I were to be given half the chance.

By a quarter before eight, I still felt tired and knew there was no hope for any more sleep. I rolled off of the couch and stumbled to the kitchen to make coffee. While it percolated, I looked outside the kitchen window at the Bahamian morning. That's how I saw the limo pull up at eight o'clock on the dot. I had not known that there was a set time for the night's activities to end, but I guess this was it.

Pouring myself a cup of the strong coffee that I had just made, I continued to watch the limo from the window. I didn't even hear Jijuri behind me, so I jumped when I felt his arms around my waist and his thin body pressed against my backside.

"Jijuri," I said, confident that it was not Marcus or anyone else in the house.

"Master Loch, thank you so much for last night," he said, even as he continued to hug and press his face into my back.

I reached down and held his hairless arms wrapped in front of me. "You are welcome. How did it go?" I chided myself for asking, but I couldn't help it. My curiosity was killing me.

"I think I am in love with you and Master Marcus," Jijuri sighed, still clinging to me tightly.

I laughed out loud before asking, "What? Why?"

"You are both what I need," he told me softly.

"Let go of me, Jijuri," I ordered, my voice firm. He complied. I twisted around. "Look at me." He did as I commanded. "You can find what you need here, Jijuri, but you must put yourself out there and try to find it."

"May I come and live with you two in the United States?"

"Lord, no!" I snorted. Seeing that it hurt his feelings, I immediately softened my tone and said, "Jijuri, we are both college students and have no money."

"I would work for you and Master Marcus," he said with downcast eyes.

"That's no life for you, buddy. You will find what you need here and you will be very happy. We will miss you and hope to come and visit someday."

"Yes, Master Loch."

I hugged the suddenly sweet Junkanoo boy to my chest and held him there for almost a minute before releasing him. The other two boys were already going out to the limo, so Jijuri followed them out as I watched from the window. We waved right before he slid into the black limo and it rolled away.

Immediately, I felt a tingling sensation on my skin and a slight twitch in my crotch. Knowing that Marcus was near, I spun around and saw him in the doorway of the bedroom. His big naked frame filled up the doorway and his arms were spread out against it, reminding me of Atlas holding up the sky. Atlas only wished he had a cock like the one I was looking at.

"Loch," he called to me.

"Marcus," I said, my voice unrecognizable it was so husky.

"Shower with me," he ordered, his voice reflecting his lust

as well.

I went to him immediately and hugged his body just as Jijuri had hugged mine. Marcus pulled me to the bathroom and into the shower. We did not say anything else to each other, but had no problem understanding what to do with each other.

I scrubbed Marcus clean, before doing the same thing to myself. He scrubbed my back and then took the pouf from me and hung it up. I stood in front of this magnificent man and was unable to take my eyes off of his. My green eyes were laser-locked onto his golden eyes and he seemed to be in the same predicament.

When he finally did break the silence, he ordered me to do what I wanted to do anyway. "Mark me, Loch. Make me yours." His golden eyes blazed at me, like a mighty fire was raging behind those eyes and the dry wind from the inferno was howling and scattering the individual grains of gold.

I didn't say a word as I lowered myself down to the shower tiles. Grabbing the root of his big mast with one hand, I angled it up towards my face, leaned forward, and kissed the tip of his glorious cock head with the softest seal of my lips I could under the constant stream of water.

Marcus moaned a deep-chest sigh above me.

Holding my man's cock up to his stomach, I took a mighty lick up the underside from base to tip, leaving a wide swath of saliva behind to watch it only be washed away with the shower water. I opened my hand and pressed his hot member up against his hard abs and held it there. Using my other hand, I lifted his big full balls and sucked them into my hungry mouth.

Grabbing my head with both hands, my football playing boyfriend steadied himself.

I licked, sucked, and pulled on those balls, feeling Marcus' cock thrum and pulse under my palm as I did. Spitting out his balls, I made my way back up to his cock and released it from the cage I had made with my palm. It sprang towards my face and I let it slap down onto my extended tongue.

Teasing just the head, I explored every part of it with my tongue, lips, and teeth. Marcus growled for release, but this was my show. This was where I was dominant and where I had the power. He would achieve his release when I was ready for him to and at no other time.

Running the tip of my tongue around Battle's mighty cock head, I moved to dip it into his piss slit and suck out the precious pre-cum that so easily flowed out of his monster. I loved how his cock head sat on his shaft with the ridge running around it, reminding me of the flange on a pipe.

Now I was ready. Without any warning, I consumed him. Opening wide, I pushed my face forward and impaled myself on his giant cock. My throat opened and he entered it. Never before had I been able to take all of Marcus inside my mouth, but this time it was mine. I would do it now, because he was mine and I would mark him as such.

I heard the sharp intake of breath by Marcus even over the pounding of the water from the shower. He must have felt the suddenly tight confines of my throat constrict around that gloriously large cock head as it entered a place it had never conquered before.

Pulling back off of him, I found the process relatively easy to repeat now that I had done it and wondered why it had been so difficult in the first place. I buried my nose into his wet coppery bush with each thrust. I found myself pausing between thrusts and breathing in deeply — smelling the musky masculine smell of my favorite person on Earth.

Marcus moved his hands to the back of my head and tried to get even more of his thick shaft into my throat. His cock had swelled even bigger with blood and he was close to his climax. I let him manipulate my head for a few more seconds before I quickly pumped my head up and down on his hard shaft until he was ready to burst.

Once more, I opened wide and let him enter my throat. This time I held him there, my lips pressed onto his pubic hair and his mighty cock completely inside of me. Marcus erupted in a huge discharge that I worried might hurt me at first. Howling, he held me in place as he dumped his load directly down my throat into my stomach.

Marcus' yell was so loud that we were soon joined by Vance and Jordan, who were checking to make sure everything was okay. I had already pulled back to be able to breathe when they appeared.

"Fuck, Battle! We thought you were being murdered or something," Vance said loudly so he could be heard over the shower.

"How does he have any energy or fucking seed left to do that?" Jordan asked, looking at Vance in wonder.

"Sorry, fellas. Loch was just reminding me why there will never be another man for me, but him," Marcus apologized.

My face burned with pride as I licked the few remaining drops of sweet man-cream from Marcus' piss hole. The boys left the bathroom still shaking their heads and I stood up, happy to be out of that squatting position.

Turning off the water, I dried Marcus and then myself before taking his hand and pulling him towards the bed. I pushed him down on it and then lubed his still hard cock while never taking my eyes off of his. He smiled broadly, showing off his perfect white teeth.

Crawling up onto the bed, Marcus helped me between his legs. Once again, we were on the same page without saying a word. He was one hundred percent positive about what I was planning and that confidence in me was so hot.

I lay down on top of my man. His hot cock snaked up the crack of my ass as my back and head took up residence on his broad chest. Marcus wrapped his thick legs around mine and hooked his feet behind my ankles. A big muscled arm clamped down onto my chest to hold me in place. Moving my ass back and forth slightly, I teased his ever-hardened joint until he growled his need to me.

Reaching under me, I grabbed my boyfriend's sticky cock, lifted myself off of him, placed his big cock head onto my tiny puckered hole, and then pushed myself back down into his crotch. Marcus sighed behind me as I bit my lip from the pain. He was my man. His cock was mine. My ass was his. This is where I wanted to be. This is where we wanted to be.

Marcus' dick never seemed to end as it snaked inside me further and further. He kept my anal ring stretched to its limits as he completely filled me up. Blazing a path of red hot destruction through my anal channel, his cock punched my prostate, bringing me waves of pleasure to replace the pain of his entrance.

Finally, we reached the end of his limits and I was completely full of him. Marcus' cock throbbed with each heartbeat inside of me and that was exactly what he was — my second heart.

I lay my head back and sighed, knowing that this was the place where I belonged and that it was perfect. I could hear Marcus' heartbeat and feel the heat rolling off of his skin, but what turned me on the most was the electrical charge between us was off-the-chart tonight. It was like our skins were full of static electricity and the sparks were flying everywhere.

I grabbed my hard cock with my lube-slickened hand and began to jack myself off. Never before had I ever been able to truly get hard with a hot cock planted firmly in my ass, but that did not seem to ever be the case with Marcus Battle. My cock was so painfully hard and I needed release so badly.

Marcus held my hips as I arched my back and pumped my fist harder and faster on my swollen shaft. I held my breath as

I exploded into my climax. Ropy strands of hot semen splashed on my chest and neck as I shot volley after volley. Seconds later, my ass muscles responded to my climax by clamping tighter around Marcus' hot throbbing cock planted deep inside me.

"Fuck, yes! That's my man," Marcus growled through clenched teeth as he began to move my tight ass up and down on his pole. He felt bigger and wider than ever as he moved into me with each thrust.

Amazed at his stamina like always, I melted into Marcus' chest and let him transport me to Valhalla. I only felt complete when he was inside me like this and his fast pace of fucking was making mincemeat of my prostate which was sending multiple pleasure signals to my brain despite my recent release.

"So fucking tight," Marcus hissed as he buried himself fully inside me and exploded with his climax. Coating my ass with his hot sperm, we both melted into each other, becoming one.

I rode his chest up and down as he tried to catch his breath. I was covered and full of cum, but I was the happiest I had ever been. Successfully marking Marcus Battle as my man, I felt totally relaxed.

"Well, that was unexpected," I said to him.

"Not for me, Loch, not for me."

"I just didn't think you would be able to do that after spending the night with Jijuri."

"Well, I aim to please you, Loch," Marcus said below me. He ran his big hands all over my body, including accidentally through my cooling cum. My man took care of that, by feeding his thick fingers into my mouth one at a time for me to clean.

I loved sucking on his thick digits almost as much as I did sucking on his fat lap-hog. Once I had Marcus' fingers clean, his hands were on my shoulders and back forcing me into a sitting position.

"Turn and face me, Loch."

I was extremely aware that Marcus' cock was still rock-hard inside of me and I sensed that he did not want me to mess with that. Deciding what to do in an instant, I slowly started to spin around on top of him, making sure that I didn't kick him in the face or hurt his manhood.

Once I had completed the one-hundred-eighty-degree turn, I sat on his lap as he raised his legs. I leaned back onto his bent legs and smiled down at my big boyfriend.

Marcus ran his hands up my chest, eventually tweaking my nipples. He looked up to me and then he stuck his thumb inside my mouth. I sucked on it until he removed it and closed my lips with it.

"What's on your mind, boyfriend-of-mine?" I asked.

"Jijuri was a good time," he said, his voice distant.

"Good."

"He could take my length, but not my width," he admitted to me.

"Really?" I asked, already feeling guilty that I had picked him.

"Yeah. It took a while to get him to loosen up enough to half fuck him."

"I'm sorry that I didn't pick someone better for you, Marcus."

His eyes blazed at me and his wet thumb went back to my lips. "Don't be. I enjoyed commanding him. He took to it like you do."

"I guess we need it."

"You do need it. Jijuri made me appreciate you even more," he whispered.

"In what way?"

"Not just the physical. You have always blown me away in

that department—doing things that no one has ever done to me before. But, now I know how important it is for me to dominate you. It is when you are the most responsive and the most free. I'm doing you a disservice not to allow you to experience that more often."

"You know me better than I know myself."

"And what you did to me in that shower today was remarkable."

I laughed and said, "I surprised myself."

"It was amazing," Marcus said, smoldering. "And that is what I am talking about, Loch. When I command you . . . when I assert my will over you, your response is immediate and magnificent."

"You do have a certain way over me, Battle," I said, my voice breathy and ragged.

"We are going to explore more in this vein when we return to Chapel Hill," he said with certainty.

"Yes, Sir," I answered, even as my cock began to harden in response.

CHAPTER TWENTY-EIGHT

Back in Chapel Hill, I was both thrilled when I thought of the things Marcus had said in the Bahamas and afraid that it would change our relationship. I had finally found someone who cared about me as much as I cared about him. We got along famously, outside of bed and inside. The two of us were like a phoenix who had literally caught fire and burned like the sun.

Marcus had a major project to work on for his marketing class in the weeks after spring break, so I didn't get to see him as much as I would have wanted. We stole time between classes for a quick fuck or I would blow him and then we would go to dinner. But, his project was over at the end of the week and he had already told me that we were not leaving the bed for the entire weekend.

"Stock up on some food, Loch. We're going to make up for lost time," were his exact words that sent shivers running through every part of my body.

I followed his orders and stocked my dorm fridge full of our favorites in anticipation. Classes dragged that day as I waited for him. Returning to my dorm after my last class for the day, I was excited to see a lively game of lacrosse going on in the quad and a bunch of my friends drinking on the bench.

Joining the fun, I hung out as I waited for Marcus. When he entered the quad, a sensation like riding on an off-kilter washing machine suddenly happened to my body. I looked up for him immediately, knowing that he was in the area. Sure enough, I saw the tall tight end as he rounded the corner of the library and continued to walk across the parking lot to-wards me, the strap of his book bag casually draped over one broad shoulder.

"Hey." His deep voice boomed as he approached the bench where I was sitting.

"Hey." I couldn't help smiling at him. He made my day whenever he appeared.

"Wanna play, Marcus?" my buddy Bob called from down the quad.

"Sure," Marcus yelled back and shrugged his shoulders at me.

I cheered for him as he played against my friends and dorm mates. He was a giant among our peers and easily moved up and down the quad like liquid mercury. Marcus was a rare combination—physical dominance and graceful style all in one amazing package.

By the time the game ended, my body was ringing like a bell with sexual tension. My eyes were full of a sweaty Marcus as he walked over to me, leaned in, and whispered into my ear, "Get upstairs, Loch. I'm going to slam you into that mat-tress just like I did that lacrosse ball into the back of the net."

"Yes, sir." I gulped, already getting off the bench and head-ing for the dorm door.

Once in the room, Marcus and I were all over each other. We fucked for the next four hours without saying anything to each other or taking more than a ten minute break between.

Marcus lived up to his promise, never really letting us out of the bed for the weekend, unless we were screwing on the couch, when I was spread-eagled on the coffee table, or hang-ing from one of the exposed pipes from the wall. By the time Sunday night rolled around, we both seemed refreshed and ready to face the rest of the month and finals week.

I was lying sideways on the bed and Marcus' head was on

my stomach. We were both sweating profusely, despite the air conditioning. Marcus had just shown me who the boss was and my legs were complete Jello jigglers. Running my fingers through his beautiful copper hair hanging over his forehead, I once again wondered how I got this lucky. I continued to explore down onto his thick chest with my fingers.

Marcus' chest hair had grown in some more this year, but it was still contained to his upper chest and his treasure trail. He looked so smoking hot and I played in it with glee.

"You do truly like my body, don't you?" he asked, seeming to still be amazed even after two years.

"Love your body . . ."

He was quiet for a couple of minutes while I continued to play with his chest hair. "Do you remember what we talked about in Nassau?" he asked cautiously.

"Yes, Marcus." I had been waiting on this since we returned from the Bahamas and now here it was.

"Would you trust me enough to try . . . some stuff?"

"Of course. There is no one in the world who I trust more than you, my man."

Marcus sat up and spun around to look at me. "Can I plan it, then?"

I chuckled at first and then said, "I guess it does need to be planned, doesn't it?"

"It does, Loch. You planned out the first one."

"Your locker at the end of football camp?" I asked, remembering the moment like it was yesterday.

"Yes." He sighed as he probably remembered the elaborate setup that I had used to rig myself in straps, spread-eagled across Marcus' locker on the last day of football camp last summer. "I will plan for the next one, then."

"Like this weekend?" I asked, already anxious to be bound under Marcus and to submit to his every command. I'm sure most people who would look onto our relationship would think that I always submit to Marcus' every command, but there were major differences.

When Marcus and I fucked, we were communicating with each other, usually physically and sometimes verbally. If Marcus was going to dominate me, he would be making all the decisions for us and there would be very little communication between us. He would be doing only the things that he wanted to do to bring him pleasure. Vicariously, I would receive a tremendous amount of pleasure giving him what he wanted.

When Marcus and I were together, we were equals. When we followed this plan, Marcus would be the Master and I would be the Servant, his sub. He would be completely in charge and I would not be his equal. His pleasure would be the only concern. My pleasure would be of no consequence.

Control was the third difference. Marcus would be in complete control and I would have none. This was the major difference for me, because I liked to have control. I had been able to control every NOMAR that I had ever met, except one — the one whose eyes I was currently staring into. Not having control was scary for me.

"Not this weekend, Loch. I have that tour I have to do with the new recruits and the next weekend is the one before finals."

"During the week, then?" I suggested.

"Not for what I have planned," he replied, smoldering.

"Oh, shit," I whispered in awe and anticipation.

His grin was beautiful when it spread across his face. "I'm thinking we should do this at the end of finals."

"Before we leave for the summer?"

"Yes." Marcus nodded as he continued to smile.

I couldn't help but copy his grin. "Can I help with the planning?"

"Are you that desperate for control, little one?"

"Excuse me?"

"You will not help me with the planning, implementation, or execution of the plan, Loch," he said firmly.

"Oh, yeah?"

"Yeah," he answered defiantly.

"Am I to play any part in this little scenario?" I asked with a smirk.

Marcus chuckled. "You are going to play a very crucial part. And you won't be allowed to smirk either."

"Oh, yeah?" I continued to smirk.

"I see someone needs to be disciplined," he said, his voice deep and lusty.

My crotch immediately started to tingle and I became aroused. "Disciplined?" I asked with a gulp.

"Yes, Loch. And I will not hesitate to discipline you, because that is what you need. And I will always give you what you need." His tone carried such weight that I had no doubt that he was telling me the truth.

I swallowed even harder and found myself unable to speak. I nodded my head to indicate my willingness and my cooperation.

Marcus stared into my eyes and said, "And you will call me *Master*."

Yes, I will!

CHAPTER TWENTY-NINE

Finals week had thankfully come to an end. I was finishing my last exam in my geography class and then Marcus and I would begin our last weekend together. I had barely been able to study for this exam in anticipation of what Marcus and I had dubbed *Project B.A.D.* We had jokingly named it *Bound and Determined*.

Thankfully, my geology class was pass or fail, so I had not needed my total focus for the final. I was positive that I had answered enough questions correctly to get the D grade that I needed and I was relieved to finally have the school year behind me, exam week over, and the wait for Project B.A.D. over. Breaking one of my own cardinal rules, I didn't even waste time checking my answers on the exam.

Marcus told me to pack a bag before I went to the exam so I assumed that we were going to his empty dorm room. His roommate, Jeremy, had already left for the summer. I was supposed to meet Marcus at my dorm.

Still zipping up my book bag as I exited the building, I failed to see the man loitering outside the classroom. I passed him and was almost to the stairwell when I looked up in alarm. It was then that I noticed that the hallway was empty except for the two of us. He wore a baseball cap pulled down over his eyes.

That's almost all that I remember. Something dark was thrown over my head and a strong medicinal smell over-whelmed me —

Coming back to consciousness, I couldn't tell how long I had been out or even where I was at the moment. I wasn't in pain, so that was a plus, but I was constricted. I could feel rope around my chest, around my left thigh, and around my lower leg. My leg that was bound by the rope was in the air to my side and bent at the knee. I couldn't see at all. Based on the tightness running around my head, I assumed that I was blindfolded.

My head was throbbing slightly and my breathing was rushed, so I made a conscious effort to try to calm myself down. Taking several deep breaths, I slowed my heartbeat and relaxed. I started to try to thank about what I knew or what I could figure out.

Hopefully, someone on campus had seen what had happened and was calling the police. Maybe Marcus was looking for me right now. Maybe he wasn't.

Snap out of it! I was not going to feel sorry for myself. I was smart and I would figure out how to escape by myself. I didn't need anyone to help me. Or, at least that is what I told myself.

I heard a door open and footsteps.

"Open your mouth," a deep voice commanded.

"Why?" I asked.

"Open your mouth or I will make you sorry." His tone was so firm and forceful that I felt like I had no choice, so I complied.

"Stick out your tongue."

I did.

He stuck what felt like two pills on my tongue and said, "Swallow."

"I don't do drugs," I said, sounding like a mush-mouth.

"Swallow!" the deep voice boomed.

"Only because it is you, Marcus, and I trust you," I said flippantly as I drew my tongue back into my mouth and swallowed. I was thrilled that I was not in trouble and that I was truly safe with my boyfriend. I was so relieved that I felt like I could cry. His deep voice would be recognizable to me even in deep space.

His hand popped my ass so hard that it stung and made a resounding cracking sound that echoed in the room. "Master," he said firmly.

"Sorry, Master," I said quickly, feeling tears well up in my eyes. My cock hardened until it was painful. I was positive that this was Marcus — my skin was tingling, his voice was vibrating through every nerve center in his body, and my nostrils were full of his masculine smell. This was my man, but he was not letting on.

"What did I just take?" I asked and received a big hand that covered my mouth as a response.

"You will not speak unless directed to. Do you understand, Servant?" His voice was so close behind me that it made the hairs on my skin stand at attention.

I nodded my head, even with his hand across my mouth. His use of the submissive title for me had me burning like I was a virgin at a nudist convention.

"This will help," he said as he removed his hand and replaced it with a foam bit that he put into my mouth. I didn't understand what was happening until I put it together that the bit was attached to the inside of a gag that he strapped around my head. Now I was blind *and* unable to speak.

Once my Master had my gag in place, he pressed himself against my back and pinched my nipples really hard. I arched my back to try to escape from him, but I was effectively held. This was my worst nightmare and apparently my wildest fantasy, because waves of pleasure were flowing across every neuron in my body.

"I gave you aspirin to help clear your foggy head, Servant," he whispered into my ear. "Your Master knows what you need and he will always provide it for you." He ran his hand lightly down my spine and onto my ass.

I could hear him walk around me slowly, the touch of his hand never leaving my body as it explored all parts of me. He stopped in front of me and said, "You are glorious in this state, Servant. You are never better than when you are helpless, unable to interfere, and unable to control. You are forced to just react and your body responds to my every command without your brain getting in the way."

Master continued to walk around me, keeping a hand on my skin at all times. When he was behind me again and his fingers lightly were touching my ass cheeks, he whispered, "I am so hard for you right now. I cannot wait to be inside of you. But, I'm afraid that you still have some lessons to learn before that time, Servant." Master had walked back in front of me now.

What the fuck did that mean?

His hand moved to my hip and pulled it backward. My torso and head tilted forward and my foot lifted off of the floor. I was afraid of falling but the rope around my chest held me up and the one around my thigh allowed my body to basically go horizontal in the air like one of those people that a magician magically raises with a sheet draped over them.

Master kept pulling me until my head was lower than my body. This rope system was very cleverly done and I relished talking to Marcus later about how he developed it. Something hot rubbed against my face and I recognized it as my Master's cock immediately.

He smelled amazing—like soap, but still musky and masculine. Moving my head to rub his big unit, I received a *whack* on my exposed ass as a consequence. This one stung just as much as the last one and again echoed in the small room. I had already decided that we were in a hotel room somewhere, because it did not smell like Marcus' dorm room.

Master growled and said, "You are not the one in charge here, Servant. I will tell you what to do and when to do it. Do you understand?"

I nodded my head vigorously.

"Good, boy. Now, I'm going to temporarily remove your blindfold and gag. Do not speak or open your eyes or you will be severely punished. Do you understand, Servant?"

I nodded my head and made a determination to follow his commands the best that I could. He removed the gag first and then just slid the blindfold up to my forehead. Master rubbed my face with his hot cock. He explored my eye lids, forehead, my cheeks, lips, nose, and chin with it. He even pushed his cockhead into one of my ears.

"You did very well with that, Servant. Your Master is pleased and will reward you now. You may open your mouth, Servant. Your Master has a treat for you," he said as he pulled my blindfold back down over my eyes. Marcus' voice was so husky and deep that I almost didn't recognize it. I was not the only one who was enjoying this scenario.

I reached out with my hands to hold his hips and steady myself, since I was basically swinging free in space, but he stepped back from me.

Whack. He had spanked me again.

Master's lips went to my ear immediately, the hairs of his beard tickling my skin. "I know this is hard for you, Servant, but you will bend to my will. You will not be allowed to make decisions on your own. You will do what I say and only what I say. If I want you to touch me, I will direct you, Servant."

I felt tears well up and slide out of my eyes. I was sure that they were flowing under my blindfold and across my cheeks. Not sure why I was crying, I told myself to get a grip.

"Oh, my little Servant," Master said deeply as he used a thick thumb to wipe my cheeks. "Your tears will not save you. Not today, Servant, not today." He chuckled at the use of our favorite phrase.

My Master must have squatted because his head was

suddenly right next to mine. "You are trying so desperately to control and manipulate me, Servant, but it will not work. It is not your fault. NOMARs have allowed you to do this to them for years and now I must re-educate you. You will release this need for control and give yourself to me before we are done here, Servant."

There was nothing in the world I wanted more than to give myself to him, couldn't he see that? But, maybe he was right. Was I holding back? Not giving all of myself to him?

"Now, open your mouth." His order was crisp and commanding.

I opened.

"Stick your tongue out, Servant." I followed his orders, my tears drying up. Something very cold landed on the back of my tongue, not the hot cock that I had been waiting for.

The cold hard pieces immediately melted into water.

"Swallow."

I swallowed the cold water.

"That's it, my Servant. I need you hydrated for your lessons," Master told me as he spooned more ice chips into my mouth.

We continued this routine over and over until one time it was his hot cock that landed on my tongue. Master shivered from the cold chill that he got from my icy tongue. I sat patiently with my tongue extended holding his monster cock that I loved having in my mouth more than any other on the planet.

"Very nice, Servant. Your Master gets really turned on when you wait for his direction. You do want to turn me on, don't you?"

I nodded slightly and awkwardly.

"Good, boy. Your tongue was made to be on my cock, Servant. You were made to service me and bring about the greatest pleasure for me that I can know. Your ass and mouth were designed with my cock in mind. Your hands were meant to arouse my pleasure. Your whole body was designed for my pleasure. You are here for me. Do you understand?"

I nodded again.

Master did hit the nail right on the head with his thoughts. I did feel that my body was here to bring him pleasure, because that is what brought me pleasure. I had often remarked on how well his cock fit inside me like they were two parts of the same puzzle, so we were on the same wavelength with this theory.

Suddenly, Master's hand was on my back and he was pushing me towards the ground. My legs were up in the air and I was almost upside down. I heard Master sit down in a chair close to me as he held me down.

"Lick my foot, Servant."

Gladly, Master.

I started to give him an exceptional foot bath, even though it was super hard without seeing him or holding onto his foot. Master groaned his appreciation as I worked my magic. When I sucked his big toe into my hot mouth, I received another educational spank and realized that he had only ordered me to lick him.

Spitting out his toe, I continued to lick, even as he switched feet and I had to start all over again. Master's big dogs were saliva-covered when he allowed my body to go back horizontal and he shoved his hard cock into my mouth.

"Master is very pleased with you, Servant. Here is your reward. You may suck me now."

I was extremely happy that I had pleased him and I sucked and licked his cock like it held the key to my escape if I could only lick hard enough to get to it.

With a mighty moan, Master pulled himself out of me and said, "Now, my balls, Servant." I could picture him holding his cock up to his stomach and his balls out to me. "You may hold onto my hips for balance, Servant."

Reaching out to grab his hips, I steadied myself. Just as I was opening my mouth to engulf his big balls, he threw me off balance by pushing me back into my original position.

"I just had a better idea, Servant. You don't mind if I change it up, do you?"

I stayed quiet because his last command was not to talk.

Whack.

"Your Master asked you a question, Servant. Give him your answer."

"No, Master."

"Good." He pushed my chest and suddenly I was falling backwards. He stopped me again at the horizontal position. "I need to dip my balls into your mouth like they were a tea bag," he informed me seconds before he did it.

Master must have been straddling my head and now he bent his knees and his ball sack landed on my lips.

"You are doing very well, my Servant. Now, open your mouth."

I followed his commands, my heart warmed by his use of the term *my Servant.*

Master dipped his balls into my mouth repeatedly until he ordered, "Suck them, Servant."

I sucked and licked those big hairy balls, savoring their musky flavor and smell.

"These are your Master's balls, Servants. They contain the delicious Master-cream that you are so anxious to taste." He pulled his balls all the way out of my mouth. "Tell your Master how much you want to taste his sweet cream."

"I live to swallow all of your hot cum, Master. I am nothing but a human milking machine to swallow all of your precious seed that Master deems to feed me. I know that Master will provide to me as much of his nut juice as he knows that I need." We were both aware that we were overdoing this little charade, but neither of us seemed to want to end it.

"Well said, Servant, and you are correct. Master will give you all of his salty spunk that you require. You will never have to go elsewhere to get what you need. Your Master will always provide it for you."

Master dipped his balls back into my mouth. He soon replaced it with the iron shaft of his dick. Based on the happy grunts from above me, Master was enjoying pushing his hard cock between my lips as he worked his muscular thighs up and down on either side of my head.

"Would my little Servant like to taste his Master now?"

I nodded and was suddenly being spun in the opposite direction, again facing down. This seemed to be a much better angle to suck Master's cock, so when he gave me permission to do it, I took full advantage. I sucked him with gusto, eventually allowing his giant cockhead to enter my throat. It was a world-class blow-job and when I felt Master spasm and expand with his climax, I realized that I also was on the verge.

Master groaned above me, pulled his cock back to the edge of my teeth, and blasted my mouth full of his salty hot discharge. I had to swallow as quickly as possible to keep from choking, not allowing me much time to savor the super-sweet vintage he was giving me.

Falling over the edge of my climax, my cum vent opened and I shot wads of gooey cream into the open space underneath me. Master immediately brought his flat palm down on the now-tender skin of my ass cheeks. This time, it was not just one hit but multiple ones that seemed to drive the cum right out of my dick until I was completely spent.

"Did I give you permission to do that, Servant?"

"No, Master," I answered around his cock. I continued to use my tongue to push pearls of his sweet cream up to mouth as I cleaned the cum off of his still-hard shaft.

"I had to punish you, Servant, but it secretly pleases your Master that you have now provided him with the tightest hole that you could possibly have for him." He lifted a bottle to my lips and cold water soon entered my mouth and easily ran down my throat.

Master pushed me back to a standing position and I licked my lips, already missing the feel of his hot wang in my mouth. My Master moved behind me and slowly pressed his muscled frame against me. He held himself there, pressing against me, while he massaged lube onto his giant joint.

His lips were back at my ear. "Your Master dreams of this moment every second that he is not with you, Servant," he said with a very breathy voice that was loaded with lust, need, and passion.

I was very aware that with my leg bound up and bent that my ass was already spread wide open for him, but I did not realize how exposed I was until Master suddenly grazed his fingertips over my puckered hole, sending shock waves running through my body like I had been struck by lightning.

"Master is very happy with your performance today, little Servant. He is willing to pleasure you before he pleasures himself," he said as he stuck three fingers inside me in one swift movement.

My back arched and my head was thrown back as I moaned, "Thank you, Master."

He smacked my ass with his free hand even as he finger-blasted me with the other one. Master continued to saw his hand back and forth inside me while he paddled my ass cheek. The pain and pleasure mixed all together inside me, creating an amalgam of the most intense and fantastic feelings that I had ever experienced.

When Master withdrew his fingers and replaced them with his huge cock head, I was past the point of being ready to be fucked hard. He ripped the blindfold off my face and entered me in the exact same moment.

My anal ring spread wide to allow him access, but the pain was still just as intense as the pleasure was. Master continued to plunge inside me until his cock was completely ensconced in warm ass flesh.

Blinking my eyes as they adjusted, I knew that it didn't matter where I was or what else was going on in the world. This is where I was supposed to be. Marcus' body pressed against mine, his giant missile firmly parked in my rear, and his desire melding with mine to satisfy us both so completely that neither of us could believe it.

And this was just the end of our sophomore year!

ABOUT THE AUTHOR

This is Crawford's third book in his series, Cageless In College. He was inspired by a trip to the beautiful campus of the University of North Carolina to write a series based on a marked man who took a different path and attended college instead of going into The Service.

Crawford Rhine is easily inspired by travelling. His series, The Romanian Chronicles, was inspired by a summer trip to Romania and Russia where he completed four books and has added some since. These books are re-imaginings of the classic movie monsters from the 1930's, updated with new twists like Dracula, Frankenstein, the Werewolf, and the Phantom of the Opera. A recent trip to Switzerland provides the backdrop for the Invisible Man, still to be published.

Crawford's first series The Master & Servant Series are inspired by sports and occupations that traditionally exude masculinity like baseball, basketball, football, acting, and being a country music star. A trip to Denmark has inspired a book on soccer still to come.

He looks forward to continuing to travel to far-away places and publishing more books in each series.

www.ingramcontent.com/pod-product-compliance
Lightning Source LLC
Chambersburg PA
CBHW070829120626
46556CB00002B/684